GHOSTLY
BEASTS

JOAN AIKEN

GHOSTLY BEASTS

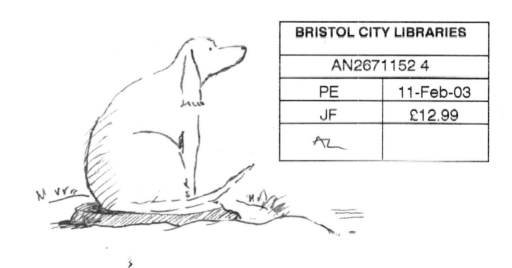

Illustrated by Amanda Harvey

JONATHAN CAPE
LONDON

This collection first published 2002

1 3 5 7 9 10 8 6 4 2

Text © 2002 Joan Aiken Enterprises Ltd
Illustrations © 2002 Amanda Harvey

Joan Aiken has asserted her right under
the Copyright, Design and Patents Act, 1988 to
be identified as the author of this work

First published in Great Britain 2002
by Jonathan Cape, an imprint of Random House Children's Books,
61-63 Uxbridge Road, London W5 5SA

Random House UK Limited Reg. No. 954009

A CIP catalogue record for this book is
available from the British Library

ISBN 0224064 63 0

'Lob's Girl', 'Snow Horse', 'Potter's Grey' reprinted from *A Goose on your Grave*, 1987
'The Winter Sleepwalker' first published by Jonathan Cape, 1972
'Humblepuppy' originally published in Puffin Post, reprinted from *A Harp of Fishbones*, 1972
'A Nasty Muddy Ghost Dog' reprinted from *Short Circuits*, 1992
'Crusader's Toby' reprinted from *The Faithless Lollybird*, 1977
'The Dogs, the Cats and the Mice' and 'The Dancers' © Joan Aiken Enterprises, 2002
Poems: 'Ducks' reprinted from Joan Aiken's school magazine; all other poems
reprinted from *The Skin Spinners*, 1976

Printed and bound in Singapore

Contents

Introduction

Short stories and poems are like mushrooms. One minute, a field full of plain grass; the next, a circle of glossy white globes that look too magical and mysterious to be regarded as food; and yet, how delicious they are! Or so some people think; other people can't stand mushrooms. And so it is with readers; some enjoy short stories, finding them just the right length for a refreshing read; while others feel terribly affronted if they have snatched up a collection of short stories by mistake 'Not a proper book at all! I want something that goes right through to the end!' And as for poems! They are worse than oysters; some people are addicted to them, while others can't even look at them without being gripped by the horrors and acute indigestion.

Most writers love short stories. A novel, a full-length novel, has to be planned, the author has to sit down and think, What is going to happen in this book? What will happen in Chapter One, Two, Three, Fourteen, Twenty? What took place before the book began? What is going to happen after it ends? And readers write in and point out hideous mistakes – the villain has red moustaches on page eleven and black whiskers on page ninety-seven. But short stories are not taken so seriously; people occasionally write to ask if Mr Johansen ever found his lost princess, or what did Harriet get for her birthday . . . But on the whole they don't bother.

Writing short stories is a completely different process from writing a full-length book; like mushrooms, like poems, short stories just suddenly happen. Sometimes they are triggered by dreams. It was a dream that gave me the idea for a poem and for a story called 'The Last Slice of Rainbow'.

Stories often germinate from items in newspapers. A man cuts down a boundary tree between two villages. The tree is irreplaceable; no punishment to the man will bring it back. The storyteller's mind begins to work on this: the man is a wood-carver, he felled the tree to get wood for his carvings. So a curse falls on him that everything he touches will turn to wood . . .

Overheard remarks are a likely source for stories: you see an ambulance backing in the street and hear a recorded voice which seems to be saying 'Watch out for reversing shepherds. Watch out for reversing shepherds.' But who are the shepherds and why are they reversing, and what have they to do with the ambulance?

Another fertile source for short stories is signs seen in the street: WATCH OUT FOR UNPROPPED BODY. Dry Riser Inlets 130 rt. 120 left. In Turkey, on the road to Troy, I saw a sign, YILDIZ OTEL. GOOD-BYE.

Or misprints: CUSTOM-MADE MIRROR TO FIT YOUR EAR. Why would one want a wing-mirror on one's ear?

Poems, like stories and mushrooms, often arrive almost complete. Or at least my sort do. I remember driving down the M1 motorway, pulling into lay-bys to get the rhymes fitted for the refrain, 'The wind is standing still and we are moving.' But

8

I read about A. E. Housman that the last poem in 'A Shropshire Lad' took him a year to write. The first two verses he made up on his afternoon walk, the third was done at tea-time, but the fourth took him thirteen tries before he got it right. A poem takes a tremendous lot of energy. Words in prose are important, but words in poems are *acutely* important.

Which stories are most popular? It is possible to guess which ones readers like best by counting the times they get reprinted in magazines or anthologies. I find that stories about animals come high in this list, and, of my animal stories, 'Lob' comes right at the top. 'Lob's Girl' is actually based on a true story that I read in an American newspaper. A girl was hurt in a street accident and her dog was found begging to come in at all the different entrances of the hospital where she was taken. The hospital was not in the town where she lived, but another one, miles away . . . I put in the ghostly bits, but you can see there was already a strong framework.

I have written quite a number of ghost stories about dogs. Which is odd, as I prefer cats to dogs. Perhaps cats don't choose to be ghosts? They are ghostly enough in real life. But I am especially fond of 'Humblepuppy' and 'Crusader's Toby' and would always want to have them in any collection of my ghost stories. Where did Humblepuppy come from? I don't know. He just arrived, like a poem, like a real ghost.

'Potter's Grey' is a real horse. You can find him in the Louvre museum in Paris. I'm very fond of him and always take care to pay a call on him when I visit the Louvre. Perhaps next time I go I'll take him an apple.

The stories and poems in this collection have been written over a span of more than sixty years. In my teens I wrote a poem every day. Now, only about three a year. And the output of stories has slowed down too. Getting the idea for a story and putting it down on paper is a wonderfully enjoyable experience – like swimming in a strong current, like going downhill on a sledge. I hope that some of the ones in this book will give the same feeling to readers.

That is what a writer always hopes.

Joan Aiken, 2002

The Dogs, the Cats and the Mice

IN THE OLD days there were no quarrels between the animals. Sheep, lions, deer, crocodiles, tigers all lived peacefully together. Even the dogs did not feel the need to chase cats. But all this changed one day, and for ever.

It happened because the dogs asked the cats to do something for them.

'You cats, you are so orderly, neat and tidy – always washing your faces and putting yourselves to rights. You are so silent and careful. Whereas we are always running about, barking and excitable. You would do this job so much better than we should!'

'But what is it?' asked the cats. 'What job do you want done?'

'It's to look after these documents for us and keep them safe and orderly. You can see for yourselves, that is no task for a dog!'

'What are the papers?' asked the cats, looking at the pile of old, old writings, paper and parchment, faded and yellow and dusty with age.

'Oh, never mind that! Will you do it for us?'

'Very well,' promised the cats, but when the dogs had gone away the cats began to think, as people often do when they have made some tiresome promise, Oh, why in the world did we agree to do that? We are busy all day, why should we take care of the dogs' belongings? The mice have plenty of time, they can keep an eye on those old papers. In fact it is probably just the kind of thing that mice *like* to do!

So the cats asked the mice to take care of the dogs' treasure; in fact they practically *ordered* the mice to do the job.

The mice were obliging little creatures, and made no objection. Months went by, and there lay the papers, and neither cats nor dogs gave them a thought.

But then winter came – week after week of bitterly cold weather, fierce wind, ice and snow everywhere, no grain or cheese or crumbs anywhere to be found. The dogs stayed in their kennels and were given bones to eat. The cats lived with the humans and were given scraps. But the poor little mice had nothing: they grew hungrier and hungrier.

At last there was nothing for it but to nibble the old documents. Paper is made from grass, and parchment from skin; there was some nourishment in it for the mice . . .

At last spring came, and now the dogs wanted their papers. They went to the cats, asking for them.

'Oh,' said the cats, 'we thought your property would be safer with the mice – they are such thrifty, good-natured little creatures! Just wait a few minutes and we will get them for you.'

But when the cats went to where the mice lived, they found that not a shred of paper was left; the mice, in their desperation, had eaten every last scrap.

Enraged, the cats began to chase the mice; and the furious dogs flew off in pursuit of the cats. And that is the way it has been ever since.

Ducks

Across the morning fly the ducks,
An arrowhead of shining wings.
I think that they are lovelier far
Than any hedgerow bird that sings.

So sweet in dawn or early eve,
Their floating pinions beating down
The surging air of autumn dawn,
Their outstretched necks all flecked with brown.

Their shimmering heads of green and blue,
Their honking calls, all seem to me
A chord of beauty and a sound
Of everlasting harmony.

Another time I see the ducks,
A long procession waddling slow
Across the muddy, small farmyard
Like dirty lumps of trodden snow.

From the school magazine, age 13

Lob's Girl

SOME PEOPLE CHOOSE their dogs, and some dogs choose their people. The Pengelly family had no say in the choosing of Lob; he came to them in the second way, and very decisively.

It began on the beach, the summer when Sandy was five, Don, her elder brother, twelve, and the twins were three. Sandy was really Alexandra, because her grandmother had a beautiful picture of a queen in a diamond tiara and high collar of pearls. It hung by Granny Pearce's kitchen sink and was as familiar as the doormat. When Sandy was born everyone agreed that she was the living spit of the picture, and so she was called Alexandra and Sandy for short.

On this summer day she was lying peacefully reading a comic and not keeping an eye on the twins, who didn't need it because they were occupied in seeing which of them could wrap the most seaweed around the other one's legs. Father – Bert Pengelly – and Don were up on the Hard painting the bottom boards of the boat in which Father went fishing for pilchards. And Mother – Jean Pengelly – were getting ahead with making the Christmas puddings because she never felt easy in her mind if they weren't made and safely put away by the end of August. As usual, each member of the family was happily getting on with his or her own affairs. Little did they guess how soon this state of things would be changed by the large new member who was going to erupt into their midst.

Sandy rolled on to her back to make sure that the twins were not climbing on slippery rocks or getting cut off by the tide. At the same time a large body struck her forcibly in the midriff and she was covered by flying sand. Instinctively she shut her eyes and felt the sand being wiped off her face by something that seemed like a warm, rough, damp flannel. She opened her eyes and looked. It was a tongue. Its owner was a large and bouncy young Alsatian, or German Shepherd, with topaz eyes, black-tipped prick ears, a thick, soft coat, and a bushy black-tipped tail.

'*Lob!*' shouted a man farther up the beach. 'Lob, come here!'

But Lob, as if trying to atone for the surprise he had given her, went on licking the sand off Sandy's face, wagging his tail so hard that he kept on knocking up more clouds of sand. His owner, a grey-haired man with a limp, walked over as quickly as he could and seized him by the collar.

'I hope he didn't give you a fright?' the man said to Sandy. 'He meant it in play – he's only young.'

'Oh, no, I think he's *beautiful*,' said Sandy truly. She picked up a bit of driftwood and threw it. Lob, whisking easily out of his master's grip, was after it like a sand-coloured bullet. He came back with the stick, beaming, and gave it to Sandy. At the same time he gave himself, though no one else was aware of this at the time.

But with Sandy, too, it was love at first sight, and when, after a lot more stick-throwing, she and the twins joined Father and Don to go home for tea, they cast many a backward glance at Lob being led firmly away by his master.

'I wish we could play with him every day.' Tess sighed.

'Why can't we?' asked Tim.

Sandy explained. 'Because Mr Dodsworth, who owns him, is from Liverpool, and he is only staying at the Fisherman's Arms till Saturday.'

'Is Liverpool a long way off?'

'Right at the other end of England from Cornwall, I'm afraid.'

It was a Cornish fishing village where the Pengelly family lived, with rocks and cliffs and a strip of beach and a little round harbour, and palm trees growing in the gardens of the little whitewashed stone houses. The village was approached by a narrow, steep, twisting hill-road, and guarded by a notice that said LOW GEAR FOR 1 1\2 MILES, DANGEROUS TO CYCLISTS.

The Pengelly children went home to scones with Cornish cream and jam, thinking they had seen the last of Lob. But they were much mistaken. The whole family was playing cards by the fire in the front room after supper when there was a loud thump and a crash of china in the kitchen.

'My Christmas puddings!' exclaimed Jean, and ran out.

'Did you put TNT in them, then?' her husband said.

But it was Lob, who, finding the front door shut, had gone around the back and bounced in through the open kitchen window, where the puddings were cooling on the sill. Luckily only the smallest was knocked down and broken.

Lob stood on his hind legs and plastered Sandy's face with licks. Then he did the same for the twins, who shrieked with joy.

'Where does this friend of yours come from?' enquired Mr Pengelly.

'He's staying at the Fisherman's Arms – I mean his owner is.'

'Then he must go back there. Find a bit of string, Sandy, to tie to his collar.'

'I wonder how he found his way here,' Mrs Pengelly said, when the reluctant Lob had been led whining away and Sandy had explained about their afternoon's game on the beach. 'The Fisherman's Arms is right round the other side of the harbour.'

Lob's owner scolded him and thanked Mr Pengelly for bringing him back. Jean Pengelly warned the children that they had better not encourage Lob any more if they met him on the beach, or it would only lead to more trouble. So they dutifully took no notice of him the next day until he spoiled their good resolutions by dashing up to them with joyful barks, wagging his tail so hard that he winded Tess and knocked Tim's legs from under him.

They had a happy day, playing on the sand.

The next day was Saturday. Sandy had found out that Mr Dodsworth was to catch the half-past nine train. She went out secretly, down to the station, nodded to Mr Hoskins, the stationmaster, who wouldn't dream of charging any local for a platform ticket, and climbed up on the footbridge that led over the tracks. She didn't want to be seen, but she did want to see. She saw Mr Dodsworth get on the train, accompanied by an unhappy-looking Lob with drooping ears and tail. Then she saw the train slide away out of sight around the next headland, with a melancholy wail that sounded like Lob's last goodbye.

Sandy wished she hadn't had the idea of coming to the station. She walked home miserably, with her shoulders hunched and her hands in her pockets. For the rest of the day she was so cross and unlike herself that Tess and Tim were quite surprised, and her mother gave her a dose of senna.

A week passed. Then, one evening, Mrs Pengelly and the younger children were in the front room playing snakes and ladders. Mr Pengelly and Don had gone fishing on the evening tide. If your father is a fisherman, he will never be home at the same time from one week to the next.

Suddenly, history repeating itself, there was a crash from the kitchen. Jean Pengelly leaped up, crying, 'My blackberry jelly!' She and the children had spent the morning picking and the afternoon boiling fruit.

But Sandy was ahead of her mother. With flushed cheeks and eyes like stars she had darted into the kitchen, where she and Lob were hugging one another in a frenzy of joy. About a yard of his tongue was out, and he was licking every part of her that he could reach.

'Good heavens!' exclaimed Jean. 'How in the world did *he* get here?'

'He must have walked,' said Sandy. 'Look at his feet.'

They were worn, dusty and tarry. One had a cut on the pad.

'They ought to be bathed,' said Jean Pengelly. 'Sandy, run a bowl of warm water while I get the disinfectant.'

'What'll we do about him, Mother?' said Sandy anxiously.

Mrs Pengelly looked at her daughter's pleading eyes and sighed.

'He must go back to his owner, of course,' she said, making her voice firm. 'Your dad can get the address from the Fisherman's tomorrow, and phone him or send him a telegram. In the meantime he'd better have a long drink and a good meal.'

Lob was very grateful for the drink and the meal, and made no objection to having his feet washed. Then he flopped down on the hearthrug and slept in front of the fire they had lit because it was a cold, wet evening, with his head on Sandy's feet. He was a very tired dog. He had walked all the way from Liverpool to Cornwall, which is more than four hundred miles.

The next day Mr Pengelly phoned Lob's owner, and the following morning Mr Dodsworth arrived off the night train, decidedly put out, to take his pet home. That parting was worse than the first. Lob whined, Don walked out of the house, the twins burst out crying, and Sandy crept up to her bedroom afterwards and lay with her face pressed into the quilt, feeling as if she were bruised all over.

Jean Pengelly took them all into Plymouth to see the circus the next day and the twins cheered up a little, but even the hour's ride in the train each way and the Liberty horses and performing seals could not cure Sandy's sore heart.

She need not have bothered, though. In ten days' time Lob was back – limping this time, with a torn ear and a patch missing out of his furry coat, as if he had met and tangled with an enemy or two in the course of his four-hundred-mile walk.

Bert Pengelly rang up Liverpool again. Mr Dodsworth, when he answered, sounded weary. He said, 'That dog has already cost me two days that I can't spare away from my work – plus endless time in police stations and drafting newspaper advertisements. I'm too old for these ups and downs. I think we'd better face the fact, Mr Pengelly, that it's your family he wants to stay with – that is, if you want to have him.'

Bert Pengelly gulped. He was not a rich man; and Lob was a pedigree dog. He said cautiously, 'How much would you be asking for him?'

'Good heavens, man, I'm not suggesting I'd *sell* him to you. You must have him as a gift. Think of the train fares I'll be saving. You'll be doing me a good turn.'

'Is he a big eater?' Bert asked doubtfully.

By this time the children, breathless in the background listening to one side of this conversation, had realized what was in the wind and were dancing up and down with their hands clasped beseechingly.

'Oh, not for his size,' Lob's owner assured Bert. 'Two or three pounds of meat a day and some vegetables and gravy and biscuits – he does very well on that.'

22

Alexandra's father looked over the telephone at his daughter's swimming eyes and trembling lips. He reached a decision. 'Well, then, Mr Dodsworth,' he said briskly, 'we'll accept your offer and thank you very much. The children will be overjoyed and you can be sure Lob has come to a good home. They'll look after him and see he gets enough exercise. But I can tell you,' he ended firmly, 'if he wants to settle in with us he'll have to learn to eat a lot of fish.'

So that was how Lob came to live with the Pengelly family. Everybody loved him and he loved them all. But there was never any question who came first with him. He was Sandy's dog. He slept by her bed and followed her everywhere he was allowed.

Nine years went by, and each summer Mr Dodsworth came back to stay at the Fisherman's Arms and call on his erstwhile dog. Lob always met him with recognition and dignified pleasure, accompanied him for a walk or two – but showed no signs of wishing to return to Liverpool. His place, he intimated, was definitely with the Pengellys.

In the course of nine years Lob had changed less than Sandy. As she went into her teens he became a little slower, a little stiffer, there was a touch of grey on his nose, but he was still a handsome dog. He and Sandy still loved one another devotedly.

One evening in October all the summer visitors had left, and the little fishing town looked empty and secretive. It was a wet, windy dusk. When the children came home from school – even the twins were at high school now, and Don was a full-fledged fisherman – Jean Pengelly said, 'Sandy, your Aunt Rebecca says she's lonesome because Uncle Will Hoskins has gone out trawling, and she wants one of you to go and spend the evening with her. You go, dear; you can take your homework with you.'

Sandy looked far from enthusiastic.

'Can I take Lob with me?'

'You know Aunt Becky doesn't really like dogs – oh, very well.' Mrs Pengelly sighed. 'I suppose she'll have to put up with him as well as you.'

Reluctantly Sandy tidied herself, took her schoolbag, put on the damp raincoat she had just taken off, fastened Lob's lead to his collar, and set off to walk through the dusk to Aunt Becky's cottage, which was five minutes' climb up the steep hill.

The wind was howling through the shrouds of boats drawn up on the Hard.

'Put some cheerful music on, do,' said Jean Pengelly to the nearest twin. 'Anything to drown out that wretched sound while I make your dad's supper.' So Don, who had just come in, put on some rock music, loud. Which was why the Pengellys did not hear the truck hurtle down the hill and crash against the post office wall a few minutes later.

Dr Travers was driving through Cornwall with his wife, taking a late holiday before patients began coming down with winter colds and flu. He saw the sign that said STEEP HILL. LOW GEAR FOR 1 1\2 MILES. Dutifully he changed into second gear.

'We must be nearly there,' said his wife, looking out of her window. 'I noticed a sign on the coast road that said the Fisherman's Arms was two miles. What a narrow, dangerous hill! But the cottages are very pretty – Oh, Frank, stop, *stop*! There's a child, I'm sure it's a child – by the wall over there!'

Dr Travers jammed on his brakes and brought the car to a stop. A little stream ran down by the road in a shallow stone culvert, and half in the water lay something that looked, in the dusk, like a pile of clothes – or was it the body of a child? Mrs Travers was out of the car in a flash, but her husband was quicker.

'Don't touch her, Emily!' he said sharply. 'She's been hit. Can't be more than a few minutes. Remember that truck that overtook us half a mile back, speeding like the devil? Here, quick, go into that cottage and phone for an ambulance. The girl's in a bad way. I'll stay here and do what I can to stop the bleeding. Don't waste a minute.'

Doctors are expert at stopping dangerous bleeding, for they know the right places to press. This Dr Travers was able to do, but he didn't dare do more; the girl was lying in a queerly crumpled heap, and he guessed she had a number of bones broken and that it would be highly dangerous to move her. He watched her with great concentration, wondering where the truck had got to and what other damage it had done.

Mrs Travers was very quick. She had seen plenty of accident cases and knew the importance of speed. The first cottage she tried had a phone; in four minutes she was back, and in six an ambulance was wailing down the hill.

Its attendants lifted the child on to a stretcher as carefully as if she were made of fine thistledown. The ambulance sped off to Plymouth – for the local cottage hospital did not take serious accident cases – and Dr Travers went down to the police station to report what he had done.

He found that the police already knew about the speeding truck – which had suffered from a loss of brakes and ended up with its radiator halfway through the post-office wall. The driver was concussed and shocked, but the police thought he was the only person injured – until Dr Travers told his tale.

At half-past nine that night Aunt Rebecca Hoskins was sitting by her fire thinking aggrieved thoughts about the inconsiderateness of nieces who were asked to supper and never turned up, when she was startled by a neighbour, who burst in, exclaiming, 'Have you heard about Sandy Pengelly, then, Mrs Hoskins? Terrible thing, poor little soul, and they don't know if she's likely to live. Police have got the truck driver that hit her – ah, it didn't ought to be allowed, speeding through the place like that at umpty miles an hour, they ought to jail him for life – not that that'd be any comfort to poor Bert and Jean.'

Horrified, Aunt Rebecca put on a coat and went down to her brother's house. She found the family with white shocked faces; Bert and Jean were about to drive off to the hospital where Sandy had been taken, and the twins were crying bitterly. Lob was nowhere to be seen. But Aunt Rebecca was not interested in dogs; she did not enquire about him.

'Thank the lord you've come, Beck,' said her brother. 'Will you stay the night with Don and the twins? Don's out looking for Lob and heaven knows when we'll be back; we may get a bed with Jean's mother in Plymouth.'

'Oh, if only I'd never invited the poor child,' wailed Mrs Hoskins. But Bert and Jean hardly heard her.

That night seemed to last for ever. The twins cried themselves to sleep. Don came home very late and grim-faced. Bert and Jean sat in a waiting room of the Western Counties Hospital, but Sandy was unconscious, they were told, and she remained so. All that could be done for her was done. She was given transfusions to replace all the blood she had lost. The broken bones were set and put in slings and cradles.

'Is she a healthy girl? Has she a good constitution?' the emergency doctor asked.

'Aye, doctor, she is that,' Bert said hoarsely. The lump in Jean's throat prevented her from answering; she merely nodded.

'Then she ought to have a chance. But I won't conceal from you that her condition is very serious, unless she shows signs of coming out from this coma.'

But as hour succeeded hour, Sandy showed no signs of recovering consciousness. Her parents sat in the waiting room with haggard faces; sometimes one of them would go to telephone the family at home, or to try to get a little sleep at the home of Granny Pearce, not far away.

At noon next day Dr and Mrs Travers went to the Pengelly cottage to enquire how Sandy was doing, but the report was gloomy: 'Still in a very serious condition.' The twins were miserably unhappy. They forgot that they had sometimes called their elder sister bossy and only remembered how often she had shared her pocket money with them, how she read to them and took them for picnics and helped with their homework. Now there was no Sandy, no Mother and Dad, Don went around with a grey, shuttered face, and worse still, there was no Lob.

27

The Western Counties Hospital is a large one, with dozens of different departments and five or six connected buildings, each with three or four entrances. By that afternoon it became noticeable that a dog seemed to have taken up position outside the hospital, with the fixed intention of getting in. Patiently he would try first one entrance and then another, all the way round, and then begin again. Sometimes he would get a little way inside, following a visitor, but animals were, of course, forbidden, and he was always kindly but firmly turned out again. Sometimes the guard at the main entrance gave him a pat or offered him a bit of sandwich – he looked so wet and beseeching and desperate. But he never ate the sandwich. No one seemed to own him or to know where he came from; Plymouth is a large city and he might have belonged to anybody.

At tea time Granny Pearce came through the pouring rain to bring a flask of hot tea with brandy in it to her daughter and son-in-law. Just as she reached the main entrance the guard was gently but forcibly shoving out a large, agitated, soaking-wet Alsatian dog.

'No, old fellow, you can *not* come in. Hospitals are for people, not for dogs.'

'Why, bless me,' exclaimed old Mrs Pearce. 'That's Lob! Here, Lob, Lobby boy!'

Lob ran to her, whining. Mrs Pearce walked up the desk.

'I'm sorry, madam, you can't bring that dog in here,' the porter said.

Mrs Pearce was a very determined old lady. She looked the porter in the eye.

'Now, see here, young man. That dog has walked twenty miles from St Killan to get to my granddaughter. Heavens knows how he knew she was here, but it's plain he knows. And he ought to have his rights! He ought to get to see her! Do you know,' she went on, bristling, 'that dog has walked the length of England – *twice* – to be with that girl? And you think you can keep him out with your fiddling rules and regulations?'

'I'll have to ask the medical officer,' the porter said weakly.

'You do that, young man.' Granny Pearce sat down in a determined manner, shutting her umbrella, and Lob sat patiently dripping at her feet. Every now and then he shook his head, as if to dislodge something heavy that was tied around his neck.

Presently a tired, thin, intelligent-looking man in a white coat came downstairs, with an impressive, silver-haired man in a dark suit and there was a low-voiced discussion. Granny Pearce eyed them, biding her time.

'Frankly . . . not much to lose,' said the older man. The man in the white coat approached Granny Pearce.

'It's strictly against every rule, but as it's such a serious case we are making an exception,' he said to her quietly. 'But only *outside* her bedroom door – and only for a moment or two.'

Without a word, Granny Pearce rose and stumped upstairs. Lob followed close to her skirts, as if he knew his hope lay with her.

They waited in the green-floored corridor outside Sandy's room. The door was half shut. Bert and Jean were inside. Everything was terribly quiet. A nurse came out. The white-coated man asked her something and she shook her head. She had left the door ajar and through it could now be seen a high, narrow bed with a lot of gadgets around it. Sandy lay there, very flat under the covers,

29

very still. Her head was turned away. All Lob's attention was riveted on the bed. He strained towards it, but Granny Pearce clasped his collar firmly.

'I've done a lot for you, my boy, now you behave yourself,' she whispered grimly. Lob let out a faint whine, anxious and pleading.

At the sound of that whine Sandy stirred just a little. She sighed and moved her head the least fraction. Lob whined again. And then Sandy turned her head right over. Her eyes opened, looking at the door.

'Lob?' she murmured – no more than a breath of sound. 'Lobby, boy?'

The doctor by Granny Pearce drew a quick, sharp breath. Sandy moved her left arm – the one that was not broken – from below the covers and let her hand dangle down, feeling, as she always did in the mornings, for Lob's furry head. The doctor nodded slowly.

'All right,' he whispered. 'Let him go to the bedside. But keep a hold of him.'

Granny Pearce and Lob moved to the bedside. Now she could see Bert and Jean, white-faced and shocked, on the far side of the bed. But she didn't look at them. She looked at the smile on her granddaughter's face as the groping fingers found Lob's wet ears and gently pulled them. 'Good boy,' whispered Sandy, and fell asleep again.

Granny Pearce led Lob out into the passage again. There she let go of him and he ran off swiftly down the stairs. She would have followed him, but Bert and Jean had come out into the passage, and she spoke to Bert fiercely.

'*I* don't know why you were so foolish as not to bring the dog

30

before! Leaving him to find the way here himself—'

'But, Mother!' said Jean Pengelly. 'That can't have been Lob. What a chance to take! Suppose Sandy hadn't—' She stopped, with her handkerchief pressed to her mouth.

'Not Lob? I've known that dog nine years! I suppose I ought to know my own granddaughter's dog?'

'Listen, Mother,' said Bert. 'Lob was killed by the same truck that hit Sandy. Don found him – when he went to look for Sandy's schoolbag. He was – he was dead. Ribs all smashed. No question of that. Don told me on the phone – he and Will Hoskins rowed a half mile out to sea and sank the dog with a lump of concrete tied to his collar. Poor old boy. Still – he was getting on. Couldn't have lasted for ever.'

'*Sank him at sea*? Then what—?'

Slowly old Mrs Pearce, and then the other two, turned to look at the trail of dripping-wet footprints that led down the hospital stairs.

In the Pengellys' garden they have a stone, under the palm tree. It says:

LOB.
SANDY'S DOG.
BURIED AT SEA

Cat

Old Mog comes in and sits on the newspaper
Old fat sociable cat
Thinks when we stroke him he's doing us a favour
Maybe he's right, at that.

The Winter Sleepwalker

THERE WAS A man called Bernard, a miller, who lived in his water-mill on the side of the Southern Mountains, just where the forests begin to climb up the steep slopes. Bernard was a rich man because his mill, built by a rushing mountain stream, was always at work, with the water pouring down and turning its great paddle wheel. Up above the water-mill was a saw-mill and down below there was a village, with houses, church, forge and pub.

Every day Bernard ground huge heaps of corn and wheat for the farmers who lived round about, and they paid him well. In fact, he had so much money saved up that he could have stopped working and spent his days fishing or playing the flute or walking in the woods. But he did not want to do any of those things.

What Bernard loved to do best was make carvings out of wood. Some of them were big, some were tiny. He could carve figures of men, plants, animals, angels, fish, snakes, demons or stars. Whenever he had a spare minute from his mill work, he would take up a piece of wood and start to whittle at it with his knife. His carvings had grown famous all over the country. People bought them to decorate houses, furniture, village halls and barons' castles.

There were no trees growing anywhere near the mill, for Bernard had cut them all down, long ago, to carve their branches into cats and dogs and mermaids and monkeys.

Bernard had a daughter, Alyss, who was very beautiful. She had gold-brown hair, and bright, sparkling eyes. She had made herself a red dress, red shoes and red cloak. When she walked in the forest, wearing these things, she looked like a blazing fire moving along among the trees.

Dozens of men in the village wanted to marry Alyss, but she said no to every one of them.

Bernard was very proud of her beauty. 'She is fit to marry a great lord,' he often said. 'I wouldn't want her to be the wife of a local lad. What do they know! They are dull, simple bumpkins. They have not seen the world. They are as thick as planks. They are not fit for my Alyss.'

So people said, in the country round about, that Alyss was a vain, proud girl, who thought herself better than her neighbours.

In fact this was not true. Alyss never thought about her neighbours at all. She was not proud, but she had not yet met any man that she wished to marry. 'He is nice-looking, but I don't love him,' she said of Mark Smith. 'He is clever, but I don't love him,' she said of Paul Taylor. 'He is good-looking, but I don't care for him,' she said of Frank Priest. 'He is strong and willing, but I don't love him,' she said of Ted Bridge. And so it went.

Every day Alyss walked in the woods by herself, flashing like a sunrise among the dark trees. She loved to be alone, and listen to the calls of birds, or the deer and wild pigs that grunted and snuffled, the foxes that barked in the forest.

There were bears, too, higher up the mountains, big brown bears who lived close to the high peaks, guzzling up wild honey and wild apples and wild plums all summer long, and sleeping curled up in their deep caves all through the snowy winter. Alyss did not often see a bear, for their haunts were a long way from her father's mill, but she was not at all afraid of them. She was not afraid of any wild creature. She had a little pipe, which her father had carved for her, long ago, when she was small. It was made of boxwood, very hard and white. She used to play tunes on her pipe as she wandered through the forest. And the birds replied to her music with tunes of their own, and the deer and hares stopped munching to listen.

Now one day Bernard came to his daughter looking pale and worried. He said, 'Alyss, from now on I want you to sleep out in the hay barn. I shall move your bed out there this afternoon. You can have plenty of thick woollen blankets, and a goose feather quilt; you can have a lamp and a stone bottle filled with hot water to keep you warm.'

Alyss was puzzled.

'Why, Father? Why must I sleep in the barn?'

'Never mind! You do as I say! And never come into the mill in the morning until you hear me start the wheel turning. In fact, I shall put a lock on the door of the barn, and lock you in.'

But Alyss could not stand this idea.

'No, no, Father, please don't lock me in! Suppose the barn caught fire? I can't bear to be locked in.'

Well, she begged and prayed until at last Bernard gave in. Instead, he handed her the barn key, and told her to be sure and lock herself in, every night, when she went to bed.

So, from then on, Alyss slept in the barn. Her bed stood among the piles of hay and she lay under a pile of warm woollen blankets and a goose-feather quilt. At night she heard the owls hooting and the foxes yapping, the deer and the badgers grunting, the otters playing and splashing in the stream. Indeed, she was happy to sleep in the barn. Often she got up, long before it was light, and went out to wander in the forest.

As for all the men who wanted to marry her, she never gave them a single thought. But she did wonder, sometimes, why her father had sent her out to sleep in the barn, as if she were in disgrace.

Now the reason why Bernard sent his daughter Alyss to sleep in the barn was this: a huge oak tree grew further down the valley, two miles on past the village, at a crossroads. For a long time, Bernard had had his eye on this tree. He longed to cut it down, to give him a store of wood for his carvings.

But the tree did not belong to Bernard. It belonged to no one person. It was a landmark tree. Hundreds of years ago it had been planted on the spot where the land of one village ended and the next began. So the tree belonged to both villages, and to all the people who lived in them. And it belonged to their grandparents and their grandchildren. It marked the edge of the land, so the villagers knew whose job it was to mend the road, and keep the hedges trimmed.

The tree certainly did not belong to Bernard.

Just the same, one night he went out, secretly, with his sharpest axe and his biggest saw, with oxen and crowbars and a cart, and he cut the great tree down. He sliced the tree into logs, and sawed off the branches, and dragged all the wood away to his storehouse. He made a bonfire of the leaves and twigs, and left the spot bare.

Now, as Bernard's axe cut through the very core and centre of the tree, he heard a small buzzing voice in his ear – a voice that sounded rather like the rasp of a saw, cutting through hard wood. The voice said:

'*You have killed a tree that was not yours to kill.*'

'I wanted the wood. I needed the wood,' panted Bernard. And he went on with his chopping.

'Very well!' said the voice. 'Wood you wanted, and wood you shall have – even more wood than you asked for. Every morning when you wake from sleep, the first thing that you touch with your hand – that thing will turn into wood. And wood it will be for ever more. And much good may it do you.'

Sure enough, next morning, as soon as Bernard woke up and opened his eyes, his favourite tabby cat jumped up beside him on the bed. Bernard stretched out a hand to stroke the cat, and straight away, the cat turned to solid wood, stiff and silent. It looked like a beautifully carved cat, one that Bernard might easily have made himself.

At that, a deadly cold fear came sliding into his heart.

Suppose, by mistake, he should touch his daughter Alyss?

So that was why he made her go and sleep in the barn.

The people who lived in the village were furious that their landmark oak tree had been cut down, and they guessed at once who had done it. But done was done; the tree could not be put back. Bernard promised to plant a new young oak tree on the same spot, he gave them fine carvings to put in their churches, and after a while the matter was forgotten. But not by Bernard. He had to train himself to be very, very careful what he touched when he woke up each day. And even so, all sorts of things were turned into wood by mistake – he had a wooden teapot, wooden toothbrush, a pair of wooden trousers, a wooden lamp, a box full of wooden bars of soap, and dozens of wooden sheets and blankets.

'What very queer things you are carving these days, Father!' said Alyss.

Bernard grew very silent and gloomy. The neighbours never spoke to him, and Alyss did not spend much time with him, because he never talked to her.

She passed nearly all her days in the woods.

Autumn came. The leaves fell from the trees. A sprinkle of snow covered the ground. The squirrels buried their nuts and curled up in hollow trees for their winter nap. The bears went into their caves and curled up even tighter for a deep, deep winter sleep.

Alyss loved the winter, when dead leaves rustled on the ground, and then the snow made a white carpet, and the shapes of the trees were bare and beautiful.

She walked when it was light, she walked when it was dark. Her eyes were so used to the outdoors that she could see very well, even in the blackest night, even when there was no moon. Bernard had no idea how often she went out at night, up to the saw-mill, or down past the village, or far away into the deep forest.

One starry night, near the saw-mill, where the piles of saw-dust were silent and frosty, for the woodmen were all far away, fast asleep in their beds, Alyss saw a strange thing.

A great dark shape was drifting slowly along, making not the least sound of footsteps on the bare, icy ground.

As it came closer, Alyss could see that it was a huge brown bear.

And this surprised her very much, for, at this time of year, all the bears ought to be sound asleep, snoring in their cosy caves.

As the bear came closer, Alyss realized that it was fast asleep. Its eyes were shut. It drifted along softly and silently as a piece of thistledown. It even snored a little.

The bear was walking in its sleep.

Alyss said – very gently, so as not to startle it – 'Dear bear, you should be back in your cave, not on the gad out here in the freezing forest! Turn round, turn round, and go back home!'

At that, the bear stopped, and stood with its great pad-paws dangling, as if it listened to her.

'Dear bear, go home!' whispered Alyss again. Then she took her little brown boxwood pipe from the pocket of her red cloak, and played a soft, peaceful tune, a lullaby. The sleeping bear cocked his head to listen, then, after a minute or two, turned his great furry body, and wandered back the way he had come.

Just then, Alyss remembered something. Her mother had once told her that if you meet a person who is walking in his sleep, and ask him a question, he will always give you a true answer. So she called softly after the slowly walking bear. 'Oh, bear! If you know – please tell me the name of the person I shall marry?'

The bear paused a little, at that, but then slowly shook his great brown pointed head, and went drifting silently on his way.

And Alyss went slowly back to her own bed among the hay.

After that, for many nights, if the moon shone very brightly, or the stars were out, Alyss would go into the forest, and find the sleep-walking bear on the move among the trees.

Sometimes she walked along beside the bear, and played on her little boxwood pipe. And he seemed to listen for he nodded his great head slowly up and down. Sometimes, if the night was not too cold, they would find a sheltered place among the moss and leaves, under some great evergreen tree, and the bear would lay his drowsy head in her lap while she played and softly sang to him.

And, each time, as she sent him home to his cave, she would ask the same question:

'Dear bear, if you know, tell me whom shall I marry?'

But he always shook his head as he wandered away.

Almost every day men came from the village, and from other villages, farther away, asking Bernard the miller for leave to marry his daughter. But she would take none of them.

And Bernard, these days even more silent and gloomy, always had the same answer for the suitors.

'My daughter can choose whom she pleases. She is beautiful enough, and rich enough, to marry a knight or a prince or some great lord.'

But one morning, when Alyss had been wandering in the woods all night with her friend the bear, she saw the mill door open, and her father came yawning from his bed. And she ran to him and knelt, clasping her hands round his waist, and cried out,

'Father, Father, I want to marry the bear, the sleep-walking bear from the forest!'

And as she spoke the word *forest*, her lips turned to wood. Her fingers turned to wood, her hands, her arms were wooden. Her legs and feet were wooden. She had turned into a wooden statue, but one more beautiful than Bernard could have carved, even if he had spent his whole life on the job.

The poor man felt as if he had turned to wood himself.

He did not bother to start the mill-wheel working. All that day he sat in his old wooden chair, staring at his wooden daughter. He looked down at her upturned pleading face, at her outstretched hands.

That night Bernard went out into the forest. For many hours he strode about, hunting and searching. At last, tired and grief-stricken, he lay down under a pine-tree and fell into a light sleep, full of sad dreams. But at dawn, cold and stiff, he woke up, and found a great brown bear standing not far off, turning its head this way and that, as if it too were searching for some lost thing.

It was a bear. It was fast asleep.

Bernard walked up to the bear and laid his hand gently on one of its huge, clawed front paws. And straight away, it was changed to wood, a massive wooden statue of a bear.

Bernard brought out his ox-waggon. He lifted the two wooden creatures, the bear and the girl, on to the cart. He took them a long way up the mountain, and put them in a cave, buried in a deep bank of dead leaves, and he blocked the cave entrance with a huge stone.

Then Bernard went away, no one knew where.

The mill stands empty now, and the mill-wheel has stopped turning, and all the wooden carvings are covered with dust.

Humblepuppy

OUR HOUSE WAS furnished mainly from auction sales. When you buy furniture that way you get a lot of extra things besides the particular piece that you were after, since the stuff is sold in lots: Lot 13, two Persian rugs, a set of golf-clubs, a sewing-machine, a walnut radio-cabinet, and a plinth.

It was in this way that I acquired a tin deedbox, which came with two coal-scuttles and a broom cupboard. The deedbox is solid metal, painted black, big as a medium-sized suitcase. When I first brought it home I put it in my study, planning to use it as a kind of filing-cabinet for old typescripts. I had gone into the kitchen, and was busy arranging the brooms in their new home, when I heard a loud thumping coming from the direction of the study.

I went back, thinking that a bird must have flown through the window; no bird, but the banging seemed to be inside the deedbox. I had already opened it as soon as it was in my possession, to see if there were any diamonds or bearer bonds worth thousands of pounds inside (there weren't), but I opened it again. The key was attached to the handle by a thin chain. There was nothing inside. I shut it. The banging started again. I opened it.

Still nothing inside.

43

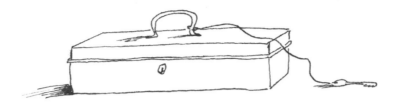

Well, this was broad daylight, two o'clock on Thursday afternoon, people going past in the road outside and a radio schools programme chatting away to itself in the next room. It was not a ghostly kind of time, so I put my hand into the empty box and moved it about.

Something shrank away from my hand. I heard a faint, scared whimper. It could almost have been my own, but wasn't. Knowing that someone – something? – else was afraid too put heart into me. Exploring carefully and gently around the interior of the box I felt the contour of a small, bony, warm, trembling body with big awkward feet, and silky dangling ears, and a cold nose that, when I found it, nudged for a moment anxiously but trustingly into the palm of my hand. So I knelt down, put the other hand in the box as well, cupped them under a thin little ribby chest, and lifted out Humblepuppy.

He was quite light.

I couldn't see him, but I could hear his faint enquiring whimper, and I could hear his toenails scratch on the floorboards.

Just at that moment the cat, Taffy, came in.

Taffy has a lot of character. Every cat has a lot of character, but Taffy has more than most, all of it inconvenient. For instance, although he is very sociable, and longs for company, he just despises company in the form of dogs. The mere sound of a dog barking two streets away is enough to make his fur stand up like a porcupine's quills and his tail swell like a mushroom cloud.

Which it did the instant he saw Humblepuppy.

Now here is the interesting thing. I could feel and hear Humblepuppy, but couldn't see him; Taffy, apparently, could see and smell him, but couldn't feel him. We soon discovered this. For Taffy, sinking into a low, gladiator's crouch, letting out all the time a fearsome throaty wauling like a bagpipe revving up its drone, inched his way along to where Humblepuppy huddled trembling by my left foot, and then dealt him what ought to have been a swinging right-handed clip on the ear. 'Get out of my house, you filthy little canine scum!' was what he was plainly intending to convey.

But the swipe failed to connect; instead it landed on my shin.

I've never seen a cat so astonished. It was like watching a kitten meet itself for the first time in a looking-glass. Taffy ran round to the back of where Humblepuppy was sitting; felt; smelt; poked gently with a paw; leapt back nervously; crept forward again. All the time Humblepuppy just sat, trembling a little, giving out this faint beseeching sound that meant: 'I'm only a poor little mongrel without a smidgeon of harm in me. *Please* don't do anything nasty! I don't even know how I came here.'

It certainly was a puzzle how he had come here. I rang the auctioneers (after shutting Taffy *out* and Humblepuppy *in* to the study with a bowl of water and a handful of Boniebisk, Taffy's favourite breakfast food).

The auctioneers told me that Lot 12, deedbox, coal-scuttles and broom cupboard, had come from Riverland Rectory, where Mr Smythe, the old rector, had lately died aged ninety. Had he ever possessed a dog, or a puppy? They couldn't say; they had merely received instruction from a firm of lawyers to sell the furniture.

I never did discover how poor little Humblepuppy's ghost got into that deedbox. Maybe he was shut in by mistake, long ago, and suffocated;

maybe some callous Victorian gardener dropped him, box and all, into a river, and the box was later found and fished out.

Anyway, and whatever had happened in the past, now that Humblepuppy had come out of his box, he was very pleased with the turn his affairs had taken, ready to be grateful and affectionate. As I sat typing I'd often hear a patter-patter, and feel his small chin fit itself comfortably over my foot, ears dangling. Goodness knows what kind of a mixture he was; something between a spaniel and a terrier, I'd guess. In the evening, watching television or sitting by the fire, one would suddenly find his warm weight leaning against one's leg. (He didn't put on a lot of weight while he was with us, but his bony little ribs filled out a bit.)

For the first few weeks we had a lot of trouble with Taffy, who was very surly over the whole business and blamed me bitterly for not getting rid of this low-class intruder. But Humblepuppy was extremely placating, got back into his deedbox whenever the atmosphere became too volcanic, and did his very best not to be a nuisance.

By and by Taffy thawed. As I've said, he is really a very sociable cat. Although quite old, seventy cat years, he dearly likes cheerful company, and generally has some young cat friend who comes to play with him, either in the house or the garden. In the last few years we've had Whisky, the black-and-white pub cat, who used to sit washing the smell of fish and chips off his fur under the dripping tap in our kitchen sink; Tetanus, the hairdresser's thickset black, who took a fancy to sleep on top of our china-cupboard every night all one winter, and used to startle me very much by jumping down heavily on to my shoulder as I made the breakfast coffee; Sweet Charity, a little grey Persian who came to a sad end under the wheels of a police-car; Charity's grey-and-white cousin Fred, whose owner presently moved from next door to another part of the town.

It was soon after Fred's departure that Humblepuppy arrived, and from my point of view he couldn't have been more welcome. Taffy missed Fred badly, and expected *me* to play with him instead; it was sad to see this large elderly tabby rushing hopefully up and down the stairs after breakfast, or hiding behind the armchair and jumping out on to nobody; or howling, howling at me until I escorted him out into the garden, where he'd rush to the lavender-bush which had been the traditional hiding-place of Whisky, Tetanus, Charity and Fred in succession. Cats have their habits and histories, just the same as humans.

So sometimes, on a working morning, I'd be at my wits' end, almost to the point of going across the town to our ex-neighbours, ringing their bell, and saying, 'Please can Fred come and play?' Specially on a rainy, uninviting day when Taffy was pacing gloomily about the house with drooping head and switching tail, grumbling about the weather and the lack of company, and blaming me for both.

Humblepuppy's arrival changed that.

At first Taffy considered it necessary to police him, and that kept him fully occupied for hours. He'd sit on guard by the deedbox till Humblepuppy woke up in the morning, and then he'd follow officiously all over the house, wherever the visitor went. Humblepuppy was slow and cautious in his explorations, but by degrees he picked up courage and found his way into every corner. He never once made a puddle; he learned to use Taffy's cat-flap and go out into the garden, though he was always more timid outside and would scamper for home at any loud noise. Planes and cars terrified him, he never became used to them; which

47

made me still more certain that he had been in that deedbox for a long, long time, before such things were invented.

Presently he learned, or Taffy taught him, to hide in the lavender-bush like Whisky, Charity, Tetanus and Fred; and the two of them used to play their own ghostly version of touch-last for hours on end while I got on with my typing.

When visitors came, Humblepuppy always retired to his deedbox; he was decidedly scared of strangers; which made his behaviour with Mr Manningham, the new rector of Riverland, all the more surprising.

I was dying to learn anything I could of the old rectory's history, so I'd invited Mr Manningham to tea.

He was a thin, gentle, quiet man, who had done missionary work in the Far East and fell ill and had to come back to England. He seemed a little sad and lonely; said he still missed his Far East friends and work. I liked him. He told me that for a large part of the nineteenth century the Riverland living had belonged to a parson called Swannett, the Reverend Timothy Swannett, who lived to a great age and had ten children.

'He was a great uncle of mine, as a matter of fact. But why do you want to know all this?' Mr Manningham asked. His long thin arm hung over the side of his chair; absently he moved his hand sideways and remarked, 'I didn't notice that you had a puppy.' Then he looked down and said, 'Oh!'

'He's never come out for a stranger before,' I said.

Taffy, who maintains a civil reserve with visitors, sat motionless on the nightstore heater, eyes slitted, sphinxlike.

Humblepuppy climbed invisibly on to Mr Manningham's lap.

We agreed that the new rector probably carried a familiar smell of the rectory with him; or possibly he reminded Humblepuppy of his great-uncle, the Rev. Swannett.

Anyway, after that, Humblepuppy always came scampering joyfully out if Mr Manningham dropped in to tea, so of course I thought of the rector when summer holiday time came round.

During the summer holidays we lend our house and cat to a lady publisher and her mother who are devoted to cats and think it a privilege to look after Taffy and spoil him. He is always amazingly overweight when we get back. But the old lady has an allergy to dogs, and is frightened of them too; it was plainly out of the question that she should be expected to share her summer holiday with the ghost of a puppy.

So I asked Mr Manningham if he'd be prepared to take Humblepuppy as a boarder, since it didn't seem a case for the usual kind of boarding-kennels; he said he'd be delighted.

I drove Humblepuppy out to Riverland in his deedbox; he was rather miserable on the drive, but luckily it is not far. Mr Manningham came out into the garden to meet us. We put the deedbox down on the lawn and opened it.

I've never heard a puppy so wildly excited. Often I'd been sorry I couldn't see Humblepuppy, but I was never sorrier than on that afternoon, as we heard him rushing from tree to familiar tree, barking joyously, dashing through the orchard grass – you could see it divide as he whizzed along – coming back to bounce up against us, all damp and earthy and smelling of leaves.

'He's going to be happy with you, all right,' I said, and Mr Manningham's grey, lined face crinkled into its thoughtful smile as he said, 'It's the place more than me, I think.'

Well, it was both of them, really.

After the holiday, I went to collect Humblepuppy, leaving Taffy haughty and standoffish, sniffing our cases. It always takes him a long time to forgive us for going away.

Mr Manningham had a bit of a cold and was sitting by the fire in his study, wrapped in a Shetland rug. Humblepuppy was on his knee. I could hear the little dog's tail thump against the arm of the chair when I walked in, but he didn't get down to greet me. He stayed in Mr Manningham's lap.

'So you've come to take back my boarder,' Mr Manningham said.

There was nothing in the least strained about his voice or smile but – I just hadn't the heart to take back Humblepuppy. I put my hand down, found his soft wrinkly forehead, rumpled it a bit, and said,

'Well – I was sort of wondering: our spoilt old cat seems to have got used to being on his own again; I was wondering whether – by any chance – you'd feel like keeping him?'

Mr Manningham's face lit up. He didn't speak for a minute; then he put a gentle hand down to find the small head, and rubbed a finger along Humblepuppy's chin.

'Well,' he said. He cleared his throat. 'Of course, if you're *quite* sure—'

'Quite sure.' My throat needed clearing too.

'I hope you won't catch my cold,' Mr Manningham said. I shook my head and said, 'I'll drop in to see if you're better in a day or two,' and went off and left them together.

Poor Taffy was pretty glum over the loss of his playmate for several weeks; we had two hours' purgatory every morning after breakfast while he hunted for Humblepuppy high and low. But gradually the memory faded and, thank goodness, now he has found a new friend, Little

Grey Furry, a nephew, cousin or other relative of Charity and Fred. Little Grey Furry has learned to play hide-and-seek in the lavender-bush, and to use our cat-flap, and clean up whatever's in Taffy's food bowl, so all is well in that department.

But I still miss Humblepuppy. I miss his cold nose exploring the palm of my hand, as I sit thinking, in the middle of a page, and his warm weight leaning against my knee as he watches the adverts. And the scritch-scratch of his toenails on the dining-room floor and the flump, flump, as he comes downstairs, and the small hollow in a cushion as he settles down with a sigh.

Oh well. I'll get over it, just as Taffy has. But I was wondering about putting an ad into *Our Dogs* or *Pets' Monthly*: 'Wanted, ghost of mongrel puppy. Warm welcome, loving home. Any reasonable price paid.'

It might be worth a try.

Snail

Snail's never had to hitchhike yet:
He moves inside his maisonette
He has no need for truck or trailer
Snail lives in jail, but snail's the jailer.

Pity him not, for, truth to tell
He's happy in his clammy cell
He has no need for shoes or socks
His lunch is leaves of hollyhocks
He has no need for road or rail
His house is made of fingernail
And in this stately pleasure dome
He travels, yet remains at home.

At night, calm cautious Snail is used
To roam, while rooks and robins roost
He greets the coming of the dawn
By winding in his shining horn;
Composed, within his gliding grotto,
'A bird in the hand' is *not* his motto.

Snow Horse

A PLEASANT PLACE, the Forest Lodge Inn seemed as you rode up the mountain track, with its big thatched barns and stables all around, the slate-paved courtyard in front, and the solidity of the stone house itself, promising comfort and good cheer. But inside, there was a queer chill; guests could never get warm enough in bed, pile on however many blankets they might; the wind whispered uneasily around the corners of the building, birds never nested in its eaves, and travellers who spent a night there somehow never cared to come back for another.

Summertime was different. People would come for the day, then, for the pony-trekking; McGall, the innkeeper, kept thirty ponies, sturdy little mountain beasts, and parties would be going out every morning, all summer long, over the mountains, taking their lunch with them in knapsacks and returning at night tired and cheerful; then the Forest Lodge was lively enough. But in winter, after the first snow fell, scanty at first, barely covering the grass, then thicker and thicker till Glenmarrich Pass was blocked and for months no one could come up from the town below – ah, in winter the inn was cold, grim and silent indeed. McGall tried many times to persuade the Tourist Board to install a ski lift on Ben Marrich, but the board members were not interested in McGall's profits, they wanted to keep their tourists alive; they said there were too many cliffs and gullies on the mountain for safe skiing. So between November and March most of the ponies would go down to Loch Dune to graze in its watermeadows, where the sea winds kept the snow away; others drowsed and grew fat in the big thatched stables.

Who looked after them? Cal did, the boy who had been fished out of a snowdrift thirteen years before, a hungrily crying baby wrapped in a sheepskin jacket. Both his parents, poor young things, lay stiff and dead by him, and not a scrap of paper on them to show who they were. Nobody came forward to claim the baby, who, it turned out, was lame from frostbite; McGall's wife, a good-natured woman, said she'd keep the child. But her own boy, Dirk, never took to the foundling, nor did his father. After Mrs McGall died of lung trouble, young Cal had a hard time of it. Still, by then he had proved his usefulness, did more than half the work in stable and yard, and as he was never paid a penny, McGall found it handy to keep him on. He ate scraps, got bawled at, was cuffed about the head a dozen times a day, and took his comfort in loving the ponies, which, under his care, shone and thrived like Derby winners.

Ride them? No, he was never allowed to do that.

'With your lame leg? Forget it,' said McGall. 'I'll not have my stock ruined by you fooling around on them. If I see you on the back of any of my string, I'll give you such a leathering that you won't be sitting down for a month.'

Cal had a humble nature. He accepted that he was not good enough to ride the ponies. Never mind! They all loved the boy who tended them. Each would turn to nuzzle him, blowing sweet warm air through his thatch of straw-yellow hair, as he limped down the stable lines.

On a gusty day in November a one-eyed traveller came riding a grey horse up Glenmarrich Pass.

McGall and Dirk had gone down with the Land-Rover to Glen Dune to buy winter supplies, for the first snows were close ahead; by now the inn was shut up for the season, and Cal was the only soul there, apart from the beasts.

The traveller dismounted halfway up the track and led his plodding grey the rest of the way; poor thing, you could see why, for it was dead lame and hobbled painfully, hanging its head as if in shame. A beautiful dark dapple-grey, it must have been a fine horse once but was now old, thin, sick and tired; looked as if it had been ridden a long, long way, maybe from the other side of the world. And the rider, leading it gently up the rocky path, eyed it with sorrow and regret, as if he knew, only too well, what its fate would soon be and what had brought that fate about.

Reaching the inn door, the traveller knocked hard on the thick oak with the staff he carried: *rap, rap!* still holding his nag's reins looped over his elbow.

Cal opened the door: a small, thin, frightened boy.

'Mr McGall's not here, sir! He went down the mountain to buy winter stores. And he told me to let nobody in. The fires are all out. And there's no food cooked.'

'It's not food I need,' said the traveller. 'All I want is a drink.

But my horse is lame and sick; he needs rest and care. And I must buy another, or hire one, for I am riding on an urgent errand to a distant place, a long way off on the other side of the mountain.'

Cal gazed at the man in doubt and fright. The stranger was tall, with a grey beard; he wore a blue riding cape and a broad-brimmed hat that was pulled down to conceal the missing eye with its shrunken eyelid; his face was rather stern.

'Sir,' Cal said, 'I would like to help you but my master will beat me if I let anyone take a horse when he is not here.'

'I can pay well,' said the one-eyed man. 'Just lead me to the stables.'

Somehow, without at all meaning to, Cal found that he was leading the traveller round the corner to the stable yard and the long, thick-roofed building where the ponies rested in warmth and comfort. The one-eyed man glanced swiftly along the row and picked out a grey mountain pony that was sturdy and trim, though nothing like so handsome as his own must once have looked.

'This one will serve me,' said he. 'I will pay your master ten gold pieces for it' – which he counted out, from a goatskin pouch. Cal's eyes nearly started from his head; he had never seen gold money before. Each coin must be worth hundreds of pounds.

'Now fetch a bucket of warm mash for my poor beast,' said the traveller.

Eagerly Cal lit a brazier, heated water, put bran into the mash, and some wine too, certain that his master would not grudge it to a customer who paid so well. The sick horse was too tired to take more than a few mouthfuls, though its master fed it and gentled it himself. Then Cal rubbed it down and buckled a warm blanket around its belly.

Watching with approval, the stranger said, 'I can see that you will take good care of my grey. And I am glad of that, for he has been my faithful friend for more years than you have hairs on your head. Look after him well! And if, by sad fortune, he should die, I wish you to bury him out on the mountain under a rowan tree. But first take three hairs from his mane. Two of them you will give to me, when we meet again; tie the third around your wrist for luck. If Grey does not die, I will come back for him.'

'How will you know that he is alive, sir?'

The one-eyed man did not answer that question but said, 'Here is another gold piece to pay for his board.'

'It is too much, sir,' objected Cal, trembling, for there was something about the stranger's voice that echoed through and through his head, like the boom of a waterfall.

'Too much? For my faithful companion?'

Cal flinched at his tone; but the man smiled.

'I can see that you are an honest boy. What is your name?'

'Cal, sir.'

'Look after my horse kindly, Cal. Now I must be on my way, for time presses. But first bring me a drink of mead.'

Cal ran into the house and came back with the inn's largest beaker brimful of homemade mead, which was powerful as the midsummer sun. The traveller, who had been murmuring words of parting to his horse, drank off the mead in one gulp, then kissed his steed on its soft grey nose.

'Farewell, old friend. We shall meet in another world, if not in this.'

He flung a leg over the fresh pony, shook up the reins and galloped swiftly away into the thick of a dark cloud that hung in the head of the pass.

His own horse lifted its drooping head and let out one piercing cry of sorrow that echoed far beyond the inn buildings.

McGall, driving back up the valley with a load of stores, heard the cry. 'What the deuce was that?' he said. 'I hope that lame layabout has not been up to mischief.'

'Stealing a ride when he shouldn't?' suggested Dirk as the Land-Rover bounced into the stable yard.

Of course McGall was angry, very angry indeed, when he found that a useful weight-carrying grey pony was gone from his stable, in exchange for a sad, sick beast with hardly more flesh on its bones than a skeleton.

Cal made haste to give him the eleven gold coins, and he stared at them hard, bit them, tested them over a candle, and demanded a description of the stranger.

'A one-eyed fellow with a broad-brimmed hat and blue cape? Nobody from these parts. Didn't give his name? Probably an escaped convict. What sort of payment is *that*? I've never seen such coins. How dare you let that thief make off with one of my best hacks?'

Cal was rewarded by a stunning blow on each side of the head and a shower of kicks.

'Now I have to go down into town again to show these coins to the bank, and it's all your fault, you little no-good. And I'm not giving stable room and good fodder to that spavined cripple. It can go out in the bothy. And strip that blanket off it!'

The bothy was a miserable tumbledown shed, open on two sides to the weather. Cal dared not argue with his master – that would only have earned him another beating or a tooth knocked out – but he did his best to shelter the sick horse with bales of straw, and he strapped on it the tattered moth-eaten cover from his own bed. Forbidden to feed the beast, he took it his own meals, and he huddled beside it at night, to give it the warmth of his own body. But the grey would eat little and drink only a few mouthfuls of water. And after three days it died, from grieving for its master, Cal thought, rather than sickness.

'Good riddance,' said the innkeeper, who by that time had taken the gold pieces to the bank and been told that they were worth an amazing amount of money. He kicked the grey horse's carcass. 'That's too skinny to use even for dogmeat. Bury it under the stable muck in the corner; it will do to fertilize the crops next summer.'

'But,' said Cal, 'its owner told me, if it died, to bury it under a rowan tree.'

'Get out of my sight! Bury it under a rowan – what next? Go and muck out the stables, before I give you a taste of my boot.'

So the body of the grey horse was laid under a great pile of straw and stable sweepings. But before this, Cal took three hairs from its mane. One he tied around his wrist, the other two he folded in a paper and kept always in his pocket.

A year went by, and the one-eyed traveller never returned to enquire after his horse. He must have known that it died, thought Cal.

'I knew he'd never come back,' said McGall. 'Ten to one those coins were stolen. It's lucky I changed them right away.'

When spring came, the heap of stable sweepings was carted out and spread over the steep mountain pastures. There, at the bottom of the pile, lay the bones of the dead horse, and they had turned black and glistening as coal. Cal managed to smuggle them away, and he buried them, at night, under a rowan tree.

That autumn, snow fell early, with bitter, scouring winds, so that from September onwards no more travellers took the steep track up to the Forest Lodge. McGall grew surlier than ever, thinking of the beasts to feed and no money coming in; he cursed Cal for the slightest fault and kept him hard at work leading the ponies around the yard to exercise them.

'Lead them, don't ride them!' shouted McGall. 'Don't let me see you on the backs of any of those ponies, cripple! Why the deuce didn't you die in the blizzard with your wretched parents?'

Secretly Cal did not see why his lame leg should prevent his being able to sit on a horse. Night after night he dreamed of riding the mounts that he tended with such care: the black, piebald, roan, bay, grey, chestnut; when they turned to greet him as he brought their feed he would hug them and murmur, 'Ah, you'd carry me, wouldn't you, if I was allowed?' In his dreams he was not lame. In his dreams a splendid horse, fiery, swift, obedient to his lightest touch, would carry him over the mountains wherever he wanted to go.

When winter set in, only six ponies were left in the stable; the rest had been taken down to the lowland pasture. But now a series of accidents reduced these remaining: the black threw McGall when he was out searching for a lost sheep and galloped into a gully and broke its neck; the chestnut escaped from Dirk as he was tightening its shoe in the smithy and ran out on to the mountain and was seen no more; the roan and grey fell sick and lay with heaving sides and closed eyes, refusing to eat, until they died. Cal grieved for them sadly.

And, day after day, snow fell, until a ten-foot drift lay piled against the yard gate. The inmates of Forest Lodge had little to do; Cal's care of the two remaining ponies took only an hour or two each day. Dirk sulked indoors by the fire; McGall, angry and silent, drank more and more mead. Quarrelsome with drink, he continually abused Cal.

'Find something useful to do! Shovel the snow out of the front yard; suppose a traveller came by; how could he find the door? Get outside, and don't let me see your face till suppertime.'

Cal knew that no traveller would come, but he was glad to get outside, and took broom and shovel to the front yard. Here the wind, raking over the mountain, had turned the snow hard as marble. It was too hard to shift with a broom; Cal had to dig it away in blocks. These he piled up on the slope outside the yard, until he had an enormous rugged mound. At last a way was cut to the front door – supposing that any foolhardy wayfarer should brave the hills in such weather.

Knowing that if he went back indoors McGall would only find some other pointless task, Cal used the blade of his shovel to carve the pile of frozen snow into a rough shape of a horse. Who should know better than he how a horse was shaped? He gave it a broad chest, and small proud head pulled back alertly on the strong neck, and a well-muscled rump. The legs were a problem, for snow legs might not be strong enough to support the massive body he had made, so he left the horse rising out of a block of snow and carved the suggestion of four legs on each side of the block. And he made a snow saddle, but no bridle or stirrups.

'There now!' He patted his creation affectionately. 'When we are

all asleep, you can gallop off into the dark and find that one-eyed traveller, and tell him that I cared for his grey as well as I could, but I think its heart broke when its master left it.'

The front door opened and Dirk put his head out.

'Come in, no-good,' he yelled, 'and peel the spuds for supper!'

Then he saw the snow horse and burst into a rude laugh.

'Mustn't ride the stock, so he makes himself a snow horsie. Bye, bye, baby boy, ride nice snow horsie, then!' He walked round the statue and laughed even louder. 'Why, it has *eight legs!* Who in the world ever heard of a horse with eight legs? Dad! Dad, come out here and see what Useless has been doing!'

McGall, half tipsy, had roamed into the stables and was looking over the tack to see what needed mending. At Dirk's shout he blundered hastily out into the yard, knocking over in his heedless hurry the lighted lantern he had set on a shelf.

He stared angrily at Cal's carved horse.

'Is that how you've been wasting your time? Get inside, fool, and make the meal!'

Then smoke began to drift around the corner, and a loud sound of crackling.

'Lord above, Dad, you've gone and set fire to the stable!' cried Dirk.

Aghast, they all raced round to the stable block, which was burning fiercely.

What water they had, in tubs or barrels, was frozen hard; there was no possible way to put out the blaze. Cal did manage to rescue the bay horse, but the piebald, which was old, had breathed too much smoke, and staggered and fell back into the fire; and the bay, terrified of the flames, snapped the halter to which it had been tethered in the cowshed and ran away over the mountain and was lost.

The whole stable block was soon reduced to a black shell; if the wind had not blown the flames in the other direction, the inn would have burned too.

McGall, in rage and despair, turned on Cal.

'This is your fault, you little rat!'

'Why, master,' said Cal, dumbfounded, 'I wasn't even there!'

'You bring nothing but bad luck! First my wife died, now I haven't a horse left, and my stable's ashes. Get out! I never want to see your face again!'

'But – master – how *can* I go? It's nearly dark – it's starting to snow again . . .'

'Why should I care? You can't stay here. You made yourself a snow horse,' said McGall, 'you can ride away on that – ride it over a cliff, and that'll be good riddance.'

He stamped off indoors. Dirk, pausing only to shout mockingly, 'Ride the snow horsie, baby boy!' followed him, slamming and

bolting the door behind him.

Cal turned away. What could he do? The wind was rising; long ribbons of snow came flying on its wind. The stable was burned; he could not shelter there. His heart was heavy at the thought of all the horses he had cared for, gone now. With slow steps he moved across the yard to the massive snow horse and laid an arm over its freezing shoulder.

'You are the only one I have left now,' he told it. And he took off his wrist the long hair from the mane of the traveller's grey and tied the hair around the snow horse's neck. Then, piling himself blocks of snow for a mounting block, since this was no pony but a full-sized horse, he clambered up on to its back.

Dusk had fallen; the inn could no longer be seen. Indeed, he could hardly make out the white form under him. He could feel its utter cold, though, striking up all through his own body – and, with the cold, a feeling of tremendous power, like that of the wind itself. Then – after a moment – he could feel the snow horse begin to move and tingle with aliveness, with a cold wild thrilling life of its own. He could feel its eight legs begin to stamp and stretch and strike the ground.

Then they began to gallop.

When McGall rose next morning, sober and bloodshot-eyed and rather ashamed of himself, the very first thing he did was to open the front door.

More snow had fallen during the night; the path Cal had dug to the gate yesterday was filled in again, nine inches deep.

A line of footprints led through this new snow to the inn door –

led right up to the door, as if somebody had walked to the doorstep and stood there without moving for a long time, thinking or listening.

'That's mighty queer,' said McGall, scratching his head. 'Someone must have come to the door – but he never knocked, or we'd have heard him. He never came in. Where the devil did he go?'

For there was only *one* line of footprints. None led off again.

'He was a big fellow too,' said McGall. 'That print is half as long again as my foot. Where did the fellow go? Where did he come from? I don't like it.'

But how the visitor had come, how he had gone, remained a mystery. As for Cal, he was gone too, and the snow horse with him. Where it had stood there was only a rough bare patch, already covered by new snow.

Midwinter Song

Hedgehog in my garden bed
do not raise your prickly head
where in safety it reposes
snug behind the Christmas roses

hedgehog in your leafy nest
let me not disturb your rest
buried in my compost heap
sleep in comfort, slumber deep

snoring in your spiky vest
sleep secure my hedgehog guest
sleep until the sun of May
warms you and you trot away . . .

A Nasty, Muddy Ghost Dog

WE HAVE A ghost dog in our family. Or we did, at least, until Grandma came to live with us. Then the trouble began.

The dog's name is Finlay. When Finlay was alive, he was a ginger-biscuit-coloured bull terrier. He was very gentle with small children. They could anything to him: thump him and roll on him and tickle him, and he loved it. He also loved food. He hated all other dogs, visitors, salespeople, postmen and meter readers, and would chase them for miles if given the chance. And he could run faster than a greyhound. My brother Greg used to exercise Finlay on his bike, pedalling flat out, and even then Finlay was always ahead.

So it was a big relief to some people, especially the postman, when Finlay got knocked over by a brewer's truck one day as he rushed out of our front gate and across the road after a spaniel that was walking along, minding its own business.

We buried him sadly in the back garden with a big wreath of dog violets and dogwood and supposed that would be the last of him.

But we were wrong. Because we soon began to hear his ghost around the house: toenails scratching up and down the stairs, heavy breathing and whines in the kitchen when tins were opened or meat cut up, loud barking when the doorbell rang, and furious growls when somebody opened the gate.

Only two people could actually *feel* Finlay. One was Grandma, who came to live with us shortly after he died.

'Lucky it wasn't while he was alive,' said Dad.

Alive or dead, it didn't seem to make much difference. Finlay, when not chasing anyone, liked to lie pressed close against the solid-fuel stove in the kitchen, on the warm hearthstone. Grandma couldn't see him there, but she kept tripping over him when she went to put on a kettle. This made her cross. It was dangerous, she said.

'You've got to get rid of that dog,' she said.

'How?' said Dad. 'Just tell me, how?'

The other person who could feel Finlay was my brother Daniel, aged five.

When he was alive, Finlay always used to sneak up and spend the night on Dan's bed, if Ma didn't find out and stop him. And – of course – now that he was a ghost, Ma *couldn't* stop Finlay.

Dan loved Finlay's company. They had agreed that Finlay could stretch across the whole bed and Dan would sleep in a loop of blanket dangling down the side.

Another thing Finlay had been keen on when he was alive was the sound of my brother Greg playing the organ.

Music is Greg's main thing. He plays the piano and violin, and he found this little old pedal organ in a junkyard and bought it for ten pounds and worked on it for months, repairing it. Now it's in our front room, and Greg had the habit of playing it after supper while Ma wrote letters and Dad read the paper.

Greg's organ-playing used to send Finlay crazy with joy: wherever he was (mostly, at that time, it would be on Dan's bed), he'd throw up his head and let out long, breathy, sobbing, boo-hooing howls of rapture – '*Oh, woo-hoo-hoo-hoo! Oh, ow, wow, wow-wow-woo-hoo-hoo!*' – which could be heard all down our street and as far away as the chemist's on the corner.

Daniel loves our brother Greg's playing too, especially one tune. The twiddle tune, he calls it. 'Play the twiddle tune tonight, Greg,' he'd say, going upstairs, and so Greg usually ended with that. It has a lot of twiddles, as you'd guess.

When Dan was a bit smaller, he used to be scared of going to bed for some reason; didn't like going up to his room and leaving us all on the floor below. But Greg's music and Finlay's company quite put an end to that; Dan would skip up the stairs and lie happy as a dormouse, with Finlay hollering away beside him and the sound of the organ coming up from below.

But Grandma put a stop to all that.

She couldn't stand organ music, she said, it was absolutely her least favourite instrument. '*Don't* ever play that thing while I'm in the house, *if* you please,' she said. 'I simply cannot endure it. Let alone the disgusting sound of that animal howling!'

The trouble was that Grandma always was in the house, never out of it, except every third Tuesday evening, when she went to her bridge club. So Dan and Finlay had to manage without their go-to-bed music.

'It isn't fair,' Dan said night after night.

Grandma wasn't even satisfied with having stopped the music; she wanted to get rid of Finlay altogether. Even his ghost. She went on and on about it.

'I don't care what you say, it's not decent,' she said. 'Having a ghost dog about the house, grunting and scratching at fleas you can't see, and growling at the vicar when he comes to call. I don't see why I should stand for it.'

'And what do you suggest we do?' snapped Ma, who had been fond of Finlay.

Surprisingly Grandma produced an idea that seemed quite practical. 'Why don't you take him back to where he came from?' she said.

Where Finlay had come from was a farm in Suffolk that bred bull terriers.

'I suppose it might work,' Dad said doubtfully. 'If the old boy went back where he was a pup . . . I suppose he might *like* to go back.'

'There'd be plenty of others for him to fight,' remarked Greg. 'He'd like that.'

None of us really cared for the idea, but in the end Grandma had her way. She usually did, because she was ready to go on arguing longer than anybody else. And Dad said (when she was up in her bedroom), 'After all, she *is* a poor old lady who can't afford a place of her own.'

Taking Finlay to Suffolk was no problem. For always, as soon as the car was parked out in front, he'd be there, ready to bound in as soon as the rear door was opened and stand on the backseat with his forepaws on either side of the driver's headrest, mouth open, tongue all the way out, staring ahead through the windscreen as if he were on the watch for snipers.

'So who's coming with me?' said Dad, rather sadly.

Ma said she'd stay with Grandma; Greg had a music exam; so Dan and I went. We sat one either side of Finlay in the back while Dad drove around the M25. Dan had his arm around Finlay, and even I thought that I could feel his warm, solid shoulder against mine. When he was alive, Dad said, Finlay was as heavy as a barrel of nails.

After about an hour, when we had left the motorway, Dad stopped at a wayside garage for petrol. Now we were getting quite close to Finlay's birthplace, and we had all three gone silent. But Finlay seemed very interested in the landscape, and we could hear him sniffing, as if the air was telling him something.

This was where we had our adventure.

Dad had got out of the car (it was a self service place) and Finlay had flumped back on the seat between Dan and me, and we were leaning against him.

All of a sudden two men in stocking masks came running, pushing Dad ahead of them (he looked startled to death), pulled open the door, shoved Dad into the driving seat, and bundled in beside him in front.

'Now, drive – fast!' said one man. 'We'll tell you where. Come on – start the motor!'

He glanced behind him, saw Dan and me, plainly reckoned we weren't worth bothering about, just a couple of kids, and dumped a heavy case he was carrying between us. It landed right on top of Finlay, who growled.

That surprised the man. He said, 'What the—' and peered about, saw nothing, poked Dad in the ribs with something he held (later we heard it was a gun), and said, 'Get on with it! *Drive!*'

So Dad started the motor and pulled out on to the road.

That was when things really broke loose.

It was plain that Finlay hadn't liked having a case dumped on him; and of course he always hated strangers at any time. Now he let out a really bloodcurdling growl and a whole hurricane of angry barks and launched himself forward like a missile.

Dan said afterward that he had heard Finlay's jaws snap together.

The man next to Dad let out a shattering yell.

'Ahhhhh! Get it *off* me!' he screamed.

Then the man beyond him gave a yell, too, and panicked, opening the left-hand door and hurling himself into the road. Lucky for him, the car was not yet moving very fast; he fell and rolled over, then picked himself up and began to run. His mate followed, still screaming, clutching at the back of his neck as if he felt teeth digging into his spine.

Dan and I felt Finlay catapult himself over the seat back and out through the open door after the men. We could see them scudding down the road. One swerved into the path of an oncoming motorcyclist. The other tripped and fell into the ditch.

Now a police car came shooting up behind us, hee-hawing away, blue lights ablaze. A clump of cops tumbled out of it and soon had the two masked men quelled and handcuffed. (One of them had his leg broken anyway.)

We learned they had stolen a valuable painting from Frame Court, a big house nearby, and the police had already been after them when they stopped at the garage to swap cars.

'It certainly was their bad luck that you had such a well-trained guard dog with you,' one of the cops told Dad respectfully. 'Where has he got to?' they asked, glancing around.

'Oh, he probably got overexcited and ran off into the fields,' Dad said casually. 'He'll turn up by and by.'

In fact, although we called and whistled, Finlay didn't come back. Perhaps, we thought sadly, he really *was* happy to be back in his old haunts.

The house, when we got home, seemed dreadfully quiet without him.

Of course Grandma was delighted.

'You see! I was quite right!' said she.

Before we heard any news of Finlay, we had a surprise. It seemed there was a reward of ten thousand pounds from Lord Frame for the return of the stolen painting, which was a very valuable one, of a bull terrier, by a painter named Landseer.

'No *wonder* Finlay didn't like having it dumped on him!' said Dan.

Dad was to get the money, though he kept saying, 'Really I didn't do anything.' But they told him that, since he had trained his fine dog to pounce on thieves, the reward was rightfully his. In the end he stopped arguing and took the money and gave it to Grandma as a down payment for a nice flat in the middle of town, where she could see her friends and be much more comfortable than she was in our house.

'Though really I'm quite all right here,' she said when he first suggested it, 'now that that nasty beast has left. Really I'm quite happy.'

We weren't very happy. In fact we were pretty miserable, and my brother Dan was just about heartbroken. He had big black circles under his eyes, and he simply hated going to bed at night.

But after five days Finlay turned up. There was a howl outside the front door one evening, and Dan rushed to open it.

'He must have been fighting all the way from *there* to *here*,' Dan said, hugging the invisible Finlay, hugging and hugging, and feeling him all over. 'He's covered in bites and absolutely caked in mud. He must have swum about forty rivers!'

The only thing Finlay wanted was to lie down on Dan's bed.

'*Honestly!*' said Grandma. 'The sooner I'm out of this unhygienic house, the better. To let a nasty, muddy ghost of a dog lie on that boy's *bed*! Why, you don't know where he's *been*!'

But even Ma wouldn't have dreamed, just then, of trying to stop Finlay. He and Dan went upstairs together, arm around neck. And Greg played all Dan's favourite pieces on the organ, ending with the twiddle tune; and Finlay stretched out, wider and wider, over the whole of Dan's bed, moaning and howling, horribly out of tune with the music: '*Oh, woo-hoo, hoo-hoo-hoo! Oh, ow, wow-wow, woo-hoo-hoo-hoo-hoo!*'

Man
and
Owl

He has trained the owl to wake him
just before it goes off to sleep
and he in his turn rouses the sleeping owl
before he starts counting sheep
and the owl lullabies him into darkness
with its wit and its woo
then owl and man snore companionably together
till the first cocks crow
only the owl's great yellow eyes are wide open
the man's like closed cupboards in his face
but their thoughts run parallel: the owl's on mice,
the man's on money
nature has organized this partnership neatly
which is not always the case

The Dancers

WHEN I WAS eight or nine or ten I used often to go and stay with my gran who lived in a cottage at Firthing-on-Sea. Firthing was a dozy little place – nine or ten small houses clustered round a big ash tree that grew in the middle of a cobbled square. There was a pub called The Dancers and a village shop run by a glum, elderly man, Mr Moon. Mr Moon was old and glum but he had in his shop anything you might need, from honeycomb to socks. The Dancers inn-sign was a picture, not, as you might expect, of ballet ladies or people waltzing, but of a bear and a dog on their hind legs, facing each other.

'It comes from the dancing bears there used to be,' my gran explained, when I first asked her about the sign. 'In those days Firthing was bigger, quite a busy sea-port; the river was deeper then and ships came across from Holland and Belgium, and they used to bring bears over from eastern Europe and Russia. Some were for the bear-baiting. People would set five or six dogs on to a bear and he'd fight them all and folk would pay to watch the show. No TV in those days. Maybe that's what the picture's about. Or, other times, bears were trained to dance. And so you know *how* they trained them? They spread a layer of red-hot coals on the ground and made the bear stand on them. And of course, poor thing, he kept picking up his feet so as not to get burned.'

'Why did he stay on the ashes? Why didn't he run off?'

'There'd be a ring of men all round with blazing sticks, or pitch-forks. They thought it was a huge joke to see the bear pick up his feet as if he was dancing the polka. People used to do terrible things in those old, long-ago days.'

Yes, I thought, and they still do, Grandmother!

Meeting her steel-coloured eyes over the dish-towel, I realized that Gran knew this too.

'Where the big ash tree is now, folk say, that's where the bear-pit was,' she said. 'And before that, according to some, witches were burned there, and, before that, who knows what people did? This was a famous country for witches once. If I'd ha' lived in those days, I reckon I'd ha' been a witch.' And she chuckled.

My gran used to help out her old-age pension by answering Questions. Neighbours came to her with their problems. She'd shake tea-leaves round in a cup, or blow flour on a pastry-board in little puffs to see what patterns it made, and then tell the people what they wanted to know. One of the things she could do was find lost belongings. Sometimes she did it with sand on a tray. 'I lost my wedding ring, I lost my best doll, I lost my screw-driver!' neighbours or their children would come crying to her, and Gran would question them very carefully: 'Where were you when you last had it? What were you doing? What were you *thinking* about?'

Then she'd take a while, it might be half an hour, it might be half a day, wandering about the house, or round the village, or maybe down on the wide, flat beach, with her hands in her apron pockets and her chin tucked down on her chest, so all you saw from the back was her grey bun of hair, untidy as a rook's nest. Then she'd go to the person who had come for help and tell them what they wanted to know: 'I believe you should look in the stable – or in the hens' trough – or the apple-attic – or the road to Ely –' and there, nine times out of ten, the lost thing would be. Once a farmer, who was the worse for drink, had lost his car, and Gran, peering into the tea leaves, told him, 'You will have to wait till the tide goes out.' For he had left it on the beach at low tide and the waves, rolling in, had covered it to twice its own depth.

Not often – just now and then – Gran was unable to find the lost thing – that, mostly, was when it was a person, somebody's husband or child. These times fretted her very much. Once it was her neighbour, Mrs Baker, whose husband had gone missing.

'Mind you, he's no great loss,' croaked Mrs Baker, half snuffling, half laughing, the way she always did, with a home-made cigarette stuck between her jaws and a baseball cap back to front on her head, 'he was a waster and a drinker but I'd like to know whether 'tis legal doings to pick up his pension.' Jimmy Baker turned up two weeks later washed up on Clettering Head, thirty miles down the coast. 'Out o' my reach, so far away as that,' Gran said. The queer thing was, he'd not died of drowning. 'Died of fright,' the Coroner's verdict was brought in.

'*Fright?* What in the world could 'a given him such a fright as that?' grumbled Mrs Baker. 'I'd 'a done it myself, if I knew how, long ago, but no such luck.'

This was after the big ash tree blew down, in the first gale of autumn, and a lot of queer things happened in the village.

School term had started, but I was staying with Gran because I'd been poorly with the measles and had a big gland swelled up in my neck and Doc Swithinbank said I needed a couple of weeks building up, running wild.

I didn't know how to run wild, so I wandered on the beach, or in the grounds of ruined Firthing Hall, or I ran errands for Gran around the village. She'd send me down to the shop, or to Mrs Dokus for a bay-twig off her tree, or to Mrs Baker for a loan of her big preserving pan. Blackberry time, it was, and I picked huge baskets of them off the brambles in the Hall grounds. That was a queer, wild place, with high clumps of briar and overgrown rhododendrons, and the lawns all going back to moss and sand. Come to that, the whole village was quiet and queer – drifts of sand covering the tar on the street, grave-stones in the churchyard buried halfway up, very little traffic, and three houses empty, that stood near the high tide mark.

'Twenty years' time from now, the sea will cover it all,' says Gran. 'Like it has already covered Endby and Hoo Holding and Salt Thorpe. They say you can hear the bells of nine churches, drowned under the sea, when the wind sets easterly. If you come back here in twenty years' time, young man, you won't find me, and you won't find this house either.'

We were in her front garden just then, where the path was paved with oystershells. I looked at the thatched roof and the beams across the front of the house, trying to imagine how it would be with waves crunching at the roof and snapping over the cross beams.

Mrs Dokus leaned on Gran's front gate, with her collie dog Skep behind her.

'Just fancy, Martha!' she said. 'Do you know what they found? Under the roots of the old ash tree?'

The night before, there had been a wild storm, and the big ash in the village square had come crashing down, only just missing Mr Moon's shop, and squashing the public phone box flatter than a postcard. (Luckily no one had been trying to phone at the time. The phone had been out of order since July.)

All morning we heard the noise of power saws roaring and grinding as men from the Highway Department worked at clearing up the horrible mess in the middle of the village.

'What *did* they find in the hole?' I asked, all agog, but Gran said at once:

'I'm not guessing. They found bears' bones. Not one. Several bears.'

Old Mrs Dokus laughed, and sang in her thin cracked voice that sometimes hit the note true and sometimes missed it altogether.

'Three wise old women were they, were they
Who went to walk on a summer's day
But one of them, she cried out in a fright
Suppose we should meet a bear tonight
Suppose he should eat me! And me! And me?
Dear, said another, we'll climb a tree
They were too frightened to stay on the ground
– But there wasn't a tree for miles around . . .'

I thought: that's a true song. For there were no trees around Firthing. The soil was too loose and sandy. The big ash must have grown up a long time ago, when the sea was farther off.

The dog Skep looked up and barked. He was a thin, bony old collie, with three legs and only one eye. In his day he had been a great fighter, Mrs Dokus boasted, would take on anything five times his size. But that day was long gone by . . .

Mrs Dokus was on her way to Moon's shop, so I went along with her, as Gran needed honey and preserving sugar and jam-pot labels.

Mrs Dokus had a white stick, and walked slowly, with Skep nudging her along in the right direction. By now the wreckage of the ash tree had been mostly chopped up and cleared away, but there was a huge hole in the middle of the village square where the tree's roots had been. The excavator truck now stood beside the pit with its jaws drooping like a disappointed dinosaur. Its work was halted while professors from the Fenwich School of Archaeology grubbed about in the cavity picking up things that looked like dark brown cricket stumps and hockey sticks. And teeth, big ones.

White tape had been rigged up all round, to stop people coming too close and falling in.

I wanted to go down and help, but they wouldn't let me. They said it was strictly a job for experts.

'Experts!' sniffed Mrs Dokus. 'If it was a bear it would ha' bit them!'

That was a saying of Gran's, when you were looking for something and it was there all the time, right under your nose.

We went across to the shop, which was on the other side of the square, next door to the pub.

Mr Moon always had a big sign outside on a blackboard: NO DOGS! And below that, PLEASE KEEP YOUR CHILDREN UNDER CONTROL!

Mr Moon couldn't abide dogs. Or children. Skep knew this and quickly laid himself down to wait, with his one hind leg sticking out and his chin on his paws. Mrs Dokus and I went into the shop.

There was a customer inside, May Hudding, with her kid, little Suzanne.

May Hudding was a thin, spindly woman with lanky no-colour hair and horn-rimmed glasses. Her husband was a sailor, always a long way off. Little Suzanne was the terror of the village. Most of the time she whined for food, attention or toys, and the sound was like an electric drill on its way to puncture your brain.

She was whining now: 'Want a jelly! Suzie wants a jelly!' and wriggling about in the small-kids' harness buckled round her chest that was intended to keep her from climbing up on the counter or scarpering off across the square.

Mr Moon's shop had a brick floor, worn into hollows from customers standing on it. The bricks were sweaty from hot damp weather. And the counter was made of thick dim wood which had gone a dim purplish colour from age. The shop smelt strongly of cheese and paraffin and sacking. There was a bacon slicer and a big red scales, and up on a high shelf were glass jars of hard sweets, pear drops and all-day suckers and aniseed balls and bulls'-eyes and jelly-babies.

'Suzie wants a jelly! Suzie wants a jelly!'

The kid was already clutching an opened packet of Lillypops – little flat candies, all different colours.

'Oh, shut up! You're not getting one!' snapped her mother, and gave the harness a jerk so that she hoisted little Suzanne clean off the ground. Kicking and roaring, the kid somehow managed to reach the light-switch by the shop door and turn the lights off. The shop went dark as a cave and Mr Moon flew into a passion.

'If you can't manage that child you must take her out of here!' he snarled.

I was by the door and turned the light on again, but Suzanne, having discovered how to do it, managed to switch it off again twice more before her mother dragged her away and out of reach. Then the kid began to yell, and her yell made the whine that had gone before seem like birds warbling.

'*Get her out of here!*'

Mr Moon's hands were opening and shutting as if for two pins he'd give little Suzanne a clout that would knock her clean out of the shop. I hadn't noticed before what big hands he had. They were stubby, like paws, and as large as dinner plates. Maybe from handling sacks of sugar and flour. Or from rolling dough out for bread. Mr Moon was the village baker too. I've heard that bakers are always bad-tempered because they always have to be up half the night, baking.

Mrs Hudding quickly paid for her groceries and left. We could hear little Suzanne's yells dying away into the distance across the square, like a fire-engine.

Mr Moon wiped the sweat from his forehead and turned to Mrs Dokus who wanted her pension cashed and a bar of yellow soap.

They talked about last night's shocking storm.

'Like the scream of a beast it was, when the tree went down,' said Mrs Dokus. 'I never heard such a sound! Old Skep out there, he jumped up on my bed with all his fur standing up on end along his back.'

'How could you see that?' I asked.

'By the lightning, of course! And then another shriek, like a yuman soul leaving its body. I went under the bedclothes, I can tell you, and took Skep along with me.'

Mr Moon pressed his lips together disapprovingly. His small eyes, set very close together, looked as if they were agreeing with each other that this piece of cowardice was both insanitary and foolish. He handed Mrs Dokus her soap and turned to me.

I gave him Gran's list.

'Rare lot of honey your gran uses,' he commented sourly, passing me the honeycomb in its wooden box. 'That's the second this week.'

'She cures burns with it.'

Several people had suffered burns as a result of last night's storm, from candles setting fire to bedroom curtains, blazing branches from lightning-struck trees, or electric appliances going wild.

Mr Moon shook his head, long and slowly.

'Waste of good honey,' he growled. 'That's not what honey be meant for.'

He hunched his shoulders together as he handed me the big bag of preserving sugar. 'Tell your gran I said that! She ought to know it. She and her folks have been in this village a tidy sight longer than that old ash tree. Since honey-dare times . . .'

His voice trailed off into a mutter so deep and grumbling that I couldn't hear the next thing he said. And I hadn't the least notion what he meant. I did not greatly care for Mr Moon, who always seemed to be blaming somebody, so I said quickly,

'Gran asks will you put it down in her book, please,' and made haste to escape with my heavy load. The shop was stuffy today and smelt even stronger than usual – a queer, rank fume, like pig-sties or greasy old blankets. Sharp. It reminded me of nitric acid in chemistry experiments at school.

Mrs Dokus was already limping across the village square ahead of me, with Skep carefully nudging her away from the white tape around the hole that had been the big ash tree's cradle and grave. The truck, loaded with branches and leaves and sawed-up bits, had driven off, and the professors with their notebooks and cameras had gone to have lunch in the pub, so the big hole was empty. I longed to climb down and take a look at what was down there, but Mrs Dokus guessed my thought and said:

'Don't-ee go a-messing about down there, boy!'

'Why not?'

'There's bad yumours coming out from that hole!'

'*Humours?*'

'Pests. That be like a plague pit that's been opened up. That wants to wait awhile to let the clean air blow in and sweep out the poison. Now, do-ee mind what I say!'

'Mrs Dokus, what did Mr Moon mean when he talked about honey-dare times?'

'Oh, mercy-me, boy, don't-ee be asking me! That be one for your gran, I should reckon. Your gran's the one who do answer questions.'

And Mrs Dokus hobbled off up Wharf Lane with Skep tugging her along the way she should go.

When I asked Gran about honey-dare times she said, 'Where in the world did you pick *that* up? Who said those words?'

'It was Mr Moon in the shop. He was in a bad mood. He'd been aggravated by little Suzanne Hudding.'

'That young 'un will come to a bad end, one o' these days,' muttered my grandmother.

'What *did* Mr Moon mean about honey-dare times? He said that you would know.'

Gran answered slowly: 'That was one thing they used to do in the bear-baiting days. Bears love honey, you know that. And they used to tease and provoke the bear by fetching out a big bowl of honey – or a honeycomb – and holding it so close the bear could smell it, then snatching it away. So as to make it angry and fierce. Village lads would jump out in front, with the honey, then away again – like they do in bullfights with red cloaks to torment and upset the poor beast.'

I wonder if the bear had ever been able to grab the honey from the boys. I hoped so.

'Once,' said Gran, as if hearing my thought, 'a boy slipped and fell on icy ground – 'twas wintertime, the puddles were frozen. He fell on the honey he was holding. And the bear, trying to get at it, savaged him so bad that he died later . . . so I heard tell.'

'What happened to the bear?'

'It got away, with the dogs after it – while they were trying to help the boy. Made for the beach and swam out to sea. Hunted creatures do that. Some dogs were drowned.'

'What about the bear?'

'Drowned too, I dare say.'

'I suppose it would be too far for it to swim home. Across the sea.'

Gran gave a grim chuckle. 'And if it did swim over the sea, it'd be too far for a bear to walk all across Europe. Of course some do say that it made off into the woods. There used to be woods here, in those days, when the sea was farther off. The man who owned the bear was roaring angry, they say. Paid fifteen pounds for it, he had. That would be a fortune in those days.'

Gran pottered about, setting her blackberry jam on the stove to bubble.

'Shall I pick you some more berries, Gran?'

'No, boy, no, thank ye, no use picking berries after last night's rain. The rain'll have washed all the heart from them. You can busy yourself writing the labels for the pots.'

While I was doing that – B.B.JELLY 19 – Mrs Hudding came knocking at the door. She was white as cheese and all smeared with tears.

'Oh, Mrs Hoadby! Suzanne's gone missing!'

She was shaking like a jelly. Gran sat her down on a kitchen chair and gave her a drink of cold water. I remembered the jelly-babies that Suzanne had roared for, and said,

'Maybe she went back to Mr Moon's shop?'

'No,' gulped Mrs Hudding, 'I thought of that. I went there – but Mr Moon'd *never* let her into the shop on her own, he said he'd not seen her – oh, Mrs Hoadby, *where* can she be? She was out playing with her toy truck in the front garden, and then she was just gone! Oh, whatever shall I do?'

'Have you told Mr Mawley?'

Mr Mawley was the village policeman. Mrs Hudding nodded, hiccuping.

'He's gone to look for her, down on the shore. But I came straight to you. Oh, please, please, can't you tell me where she's got to?'

Gran took a teacup off its hook on the dresser, and dripped into it two drops of the blackberry brew in the preserving pan, which was now beginning to skin over and turn thick and gluey. Then she tilted the cup this way and that, so that lines of dark red began to criss-cross on the white surface.

I saw her frown.

I knew she liked to be alone with any person whose question she was trying to answer, so I said, 'I'll go and take a look in the Hall grounds, shall I, Gran? Maybe Suzanne's gone there.'

'Yes, do, boy, you do that,' Gran said absently, never taking her eyes from the cup, so I ran off.

There were no people about. They were probably all down on the shore; that was always the first place to look when somebody went missing.

Moon's shop was shut, I noticed.

Then I remembered that it was Wednesday, early closing.

Firthing Old Park had two entrances, one in the village, one opening on to the beach road. The moss-grown drive leading to the village ended at a broken white gate, half off its hinges, never closed. On the gate was half a sign:

ING
ALL

Gran had told me that *firth* in the Saxon language meant a river or piece of water opening into the sea. And *ing* was a meadow near the sea. There are a lot of *ing* place names up and down that coast, Clamping, Woolmering, Walling, Iping, Hayling and Easting. More under the sea, probably.

I thought of the bear, swimming out through the waves, farther and farther, to get away from his pursuers. His coat would be matted with wet, his heavy paws slapping the salt water . . .

Just outside the broken gate of the Old Park was a splash of white paint on the tarred road. It looked as if somebody had dropped a spray-can which had burst, showering white drops all over the road surface. This must have happened some time ago. The paint was dry. It reminded me of a picture sent back by a space-craft of a star exploding. Right in the middle of the white, like the yellow heart of a daisy, was a butter-coloured shining dot.

I picked it up. It was a hard sweet like the ones that Suzanne had been clutching in their plastic tube when Mrs Hudding dragged her out of the shop. Lillypops. Of course they were common enough – all the small kids ate them at one time or another because they were bright-coloured and cheap, only 30p a packet – but still, it could not have been lying there too long, some bird or squirrel would have gone off with it.

I went on into the silent grounds of Firthing Hall.

The afternoon was closing in. Dusk fell sooner, these late-summer days, and a thin fog had crept up from the sea which reduced visibility. Of course I knew the park pretty well, by now, from all my blackberry-picking excursions, and had made my own runways among the big mist-wrapped clumps of laurel and rhododendron, and the knee-high growth of blackberry bramble.

A red sun was just sinking behind the gappy ruins of the old hall.

In the distance I could hear the waves whispering on the shore.

'Suzanne!' I shouted loudly. 'Suzanne! Are you here!'

But I didn't care for the sound of my own voice in the quiet, empty park, and wished that I had not shouted.

Anyway nobody answered.

Then it seemed to me that I heard a soft grunt. *Errukh.* Followed by a lot more silence. I stood still, with my heart thumping so loud that I thought I could hear it.

Errunhk.

Errunhk. A businesslike, contented sound.

After that, silence again.

Next I began to think I could hear a rustling and shuffling

somewhere not far off among the bushes. As if something were moving along. Not very loud – not as if something were moving *fast* – but just trundling quietly along on its own affairs, coming perhaps in my direction. Something very big. But something that was able to move through the bushes without making a lot of noise.

Suddenly I couldn't stay in the park for another minute.

I started back the way I had come, slowly at first, taking great care not to make a sound. Then panic grabbed me, and I ended up racing as fast as my legs would carry me. Outside the broken gate I stopped, though, for a moment, realizing that, somewhere along the way, I had dropped the little yellow Lillypop candy. I'd never be able to find it again. Looking at the paint-spattered patch of road where it had lain I saw, what certainly had not been there before, a huge footprint. In the dry paint. Fan-shaped, it was, with five toes, and there were five deep gouges in the tar. They looked as if they had been made by *claws*.

I ran on, gasping, as far as Gran's house. There I found the door open, and a lamp lit, but no Gran; instead, to my deep surprise, Mrs Baker and Mrs Dokus were sitting by the kitchen fire, deep in low-voiced conversation.

'Funny, isn't it, how it all comes back?'

'The way they used to dance round, and then they wrung its neck.'

'And after that they had a big barbecue and roasted it.'

'And the woman who had brought it up from a cub—'

'She'd be away outside the group, sitting under a tree and crying.'

'And after it was all eaten up they shot arrows into the sea—'

'Asking the dead spirit to take a message to the Great Ones in the next world—'

'To say they were still friends—'

'Had always been friends—'

'And loved it—'

'And done it all for the best.'

The two old women turned and looked at me for the first time.

'Where's Gran?' I gulped.

'Down on the shore.'

'Gathering her thoughts.'

'But I don't think Suzanne's there! I think she went into the Old Park.'

'That don't matter. She won't be found. She's lost and gone,' they both said together.

'How do you know that?' I said; though I believed them. But they did not answer my question.

'There's been other things lost, besides Suzanne,' said Mrs Baker.

'What?'

Suddenly I noticed a queer thing. The front door, which had been wide open when I ran into the house, seemed to have been smashed in, as if it had been kicked, or thumped with a mallet. The broken latch dangled from its fixings. And the new wooden container of honeycomb, which I had left on the dresser, had been pulled open and the honeycomb was gone from inside.

'Someone took Gran's honey.'

'That's not the whole,' said Mrs Dokus. 'My Skep's gone missing.'

'*Skep's gone?*'

'*And* my glasses,' grumbled Mrs Baker, as if that loss was far more important. Well, it was, to her, I supposed. Without them she could hardly see across the room.

'And Mr Moon's nowhere to be found.'

That seemed no great matter to me – nor did the old ladies' losses – beside the stark terror that I had felt, the sounds I had heard – or thought I had heard – in the Old Park.

I said vaguely, 'Perhaps Mr Moon took the bus to Dunwich. After all, it's early closing—'

I stopped what I was saying, because Gran had come in. She was paper-white and moved very slowly, as if walking hurt her bones. But when her friends hurried to help her, she shook her head. She said:

'Ag. Lil. We got work to do.'

'Where?' they both said.

'Here.'

Gran's piercing grey eyes swept the kitchen. They took in the stolen honeycomb and the broken latch. She nodded as if these things were to be reckoned. Then she looked at me.

'You, boy. You best go to bed. You got no part in this.'

'*Oh, Gran!*' I began. But the look on three wrinkled faces floored me. I crept off up the steep stairs and huddled myself into bed, shivering, not with cold, but at the thought of a huge dark shape making its way silently among the bramble-clumps and thickets of Firthing Old Park.

*

I thought I would never get to sleep, but in fact I went off almost at once, perhaps because last night had been such a disturbed one, with the terrible storm and the falling ash tree.

At once I began to dream.

I dreamed that the great ash tree was back in its place in the middle of the village square.

But it was burning. Flames poured and flickered up its trunk and along its branches. I could hear the flames roar. But what seemed queer, even in my dream, was that, however fiercely they roared, they did not consume the tree.

In the tree perched the three old women in their black dresses – Gran and her two friends. They were singing and chanting. I could catch some of their words.

'Take our message to the Great Ones, where the trees grow so tall that they touch the sky. Tell them that we loved you. We had no ill will against you. We needed your death. And we give you a death in return.'

A misty circle of people danced round the tree down below, with dogs leaping and bounding among them. They moved rather stiffly and cumbrously under the licking tongues of flame, lifting their heavy feet from the ground, raising and lowering their short stubby arms.

Were they men? Or something bigger and clumsier?

One of them stumped across to the tree and stood beside its burning trunk. He leaned back and looked up at Gran, who sat in a nest of flames above him, looking down.

I could see his face, lit by the fire. It was Mr Moon. But he had changed since I bought the honey and sugar in his shop. His face had darkened and his nose had lengthened and broadened into a snout.

'What have *you* lost?' Gran asked him. 'You poor thing, what have you lost?'

He grunted out some reply that I failed to catch.

But she asked him again, twice more, and the third time I heard his answer.

'I lost my way. My way home.'

'Ah,' said Gran. 'That's a hard one. But I'll see what can be done.'

She began looking up at the flames in the tree as if they were tea-leaves in a cup or grains of sand on a tray; then they started to whirl and spiral in a pattern that sent me deeper into sleep, out of the reach of dreams.

And when I woke again, it was plain daylight.

I could hear voices downstairs, so I dressed quickly and ran down. Gran was there, and with her was Mr Aldby the joiner, who was taking a look at the broken latch on the door.

'I can have that mended for you in a trice,' he was saying. 'But it sure foxes me how it got busted that bad. Somebody must 'a given it a fair swinger.'

'Have they found little Suzanne?' I asked.

Gran shook her head.

I wondered if she had been to bed at all. Her face looked, not exactly older, but drawn and withered, like a last season's walnut. Then I saw Mrs Baker and Mrs Dokus sitting at the kitchen table with cups of tea. Like Gran, they seemed weary and low-spirited.

I didn't dare ask any questions after I had seen their faces, but Gran said, 'They found Suzanne's sandal down on the shore. And, half a mile farther along, at Wansea Point, they found Mr Moon's clothes, hung over a breakwater.'

'Was he—? What—?'

Gran shook her head. 'It's no use asking. Those are questions that can't be answered. Not by me.'

You could have last night, I thought. From the flames on the tree.

But I kept quiet. I saw Gran's eyes, looking past me, widen in surprise.

'Well dang me!' said Mr Aldby. 'Look there!'

We all looked out of the open door.

Up the front path of oyster shells, dead weary and lame, hobbled the collie dog Skep. And in his mouth he carried a pair of glasses.

Thirty days later, the body of a Siberian bear was washed up on Clettering Strand.

But little Suzanne was never found.

Potter's Grey

THEY WERE HURRYING through the cold, windy streets of Paris to the Louvre Museum – young Grig Rainborrow and the au pair girl, Anna. They visited the Louvre two or three times every week. Grig would far rather have gone to one of the parks, or walked along by the river, but Anna had an arrangement to meet her boyfriend, Eugène, in the Louvre; so that was where they went.

Alongside one of the big main galleries, where hung huge pictures of battles and shipwrecks and coronations, there ran a linked series of much smaller rooms containing smaller pictures; here visitors seldom troubled to go; often the little, rather dark rooms would be empty and quiet for half-hours at a time. Anna and Eugène liked to sit side by side, holding hands, on a couple of stiff upright metal chairs, while Grig had leave to roam at will through the nest of little rooms; though Anna tended to get fidgety if he wandered too far away, and would call him back in a cross voice: 'Grig! Grig, where are you? Where have you got to? Come back here now!' She worried about kidnappers, because of the importance of Grig's father, Sir Mark. Grig would then trail back reluctantly, and Eugène would grin at him, a wide, unkind grin, and say, 'Venez vite, petit mouton!' Grig did not like being called a sheep, and he detested Eugène, who had large untrustworthy mocking black eyes, like olives; they were set so far apart in his face that they seemed able to see round the back of his head; and he had a wide, oddly shaped mouth, his curling lips were thick and strongly curved like the crusts of farmhouse bread, and his mouth was always twisting about, it never kept still. Grig had once made some drawings of Eugène's mouth, but they looked so nasty that he tore them up before Anna could see them; he thought they might make her angry.

'Hurry up!' said Anna, jerking at Grig's hand. 'We're going to be late. Eugène will be waiting, he'll be annoyed.' Grig did not see why it would hurt Eugène to wait a few minutes, he never seemed to have anything to do but meet Anna in the Louvre Museum. That was where they had met in the first place.

Standing waiting to cross the Rue de Rivoli at a traffic light, Grig was sorry that he lacked the courage to say, 'Why do we have to meet hateful Eugène almost every day?'

But he knew that his courage was not up to that. Anna could be quite fierce. She had intense blue eyes the colour of marbles; they weren't very good for observing. Grig noticed a million more things than Anna did, he was always saying, 'Look, Anna—' and she would say, 'Oh, never mind that! Come along!' but the stare of her eyes was so piercing when she lost her temper, they were like two gimlets boring right through him, and she had such a way of hissing, 'You *stupid* child!' making him feel pulpy, breathless and flattened, that he did not say what he felt about Eugène. He kept quiet and waited for the lights to change, while French traffic poured furiously past in a torrent of steel, rubber and glass.

'Come on – there's a gap – we can go,' said Anna, and jerked at Grig's hand again.

They hurled themselves out, in company with a French girl who had a small child in a pushchair and, bounding on the end of his lead, a large Alsatian dog that she could only just control; as they crossed, the pushchair veered one way, the dog tugged the other, it seemed amazing that the trio had survived among the traffic up to this day. A tall thin white-haired man in pink-tinted glasses observed their plight, and turned to give the girl a helping hand with her wayward pushchair; a sharp gust of wind blew just at that moment, the dog tugged, the pushchair swerved crazily, and the pink-tinged glasses were jerked off the man's face to spin away into the middle of the road, just as a new wave of traffic surged forwards.

With a cry of anguish, the white-haired man tilted the pushchair on to the pavement, hurriedly passing its handle into the mother's grasp, and then turned back to retrieve his glasses. Too late – and a terrible mistake: a motorcyclist, twisting aside to avoid him, collided with a taxi, and a Citroën following too close behind the cycle struck the elderly man on the shoulder and flung him on to the sidewalk, where he lay on his face without moving.

If he had been wearing his glasses at that moment, they would have been smashed, Grig thought.

The mother with the pushchair let out a horrified wail: 'Oh, oh, c'est le vieux Professeur Bercy!' and she ran to kneel by him, while, out in the road, all was confusion, with brakes squawking and horns braying, and a general tangle and snarl of traffic coming too suddenly to a stop.

Police, blowing their whistles, were on the spot in no time – there are always plenty of police near the Louvre.

'Come along, Grig!' snapped Anna. 'We don't want to get mixed up in all this, your father wouldn't be a bit pleased—' For Sir Mark, Grig's father, was the British Ambassador in Paris. But it wasn't easy to get away; already the police were swarming round, asking everybody there if they had seen the accident.

'Oh, I do *hope* the poor man is not badly hurt!' cried the distraught young mother. 'It is Professor Bercy, the physicist – I have often seen his face in the papers and on TV – it was so kind of him to take my baby carriage – oh it will be terrible if he is badly injured and all because he stopped to help me—'

A gendarme was talking to Anna, and, while she snappishly but accurately gave an account of what had happened,

Grig slipped out into the street and picked up the professor's glasses, which he had noticed lying – astonishingly, quite unharmed – about six feet out from the edge of the road, among a glittering sprinkle of somebody's smashed windscreen.

'*Grig! Will* you come out of there!' yelled Anna, turning from the cop to see where he had got to, and she yanked his arm and hustled him away in the direction of the Louvre entrance, across the big quadrangle, before he could do anything about giving the pink-tinged glasses to one of the policemen.

'But I've got these—'

'Oh, who cares? The man's probably dead, he won't want them again. If he hears that you got mixed up in a street accident your father will be hopping mad. And Eugène will be upset – he'll be wondering where we've got to.'

It seemed to Grig that the last of these three statements was the real reason why Anna didn't want to hang about on the scene of the accident. He pulled back from her grasp and twisted his head round to see if an ambulance had arrived yet; yes, there it went, shooting across the end of the square with flashing lights. So at least the poor man would soon be in hospital.

Well, it was true that if he was unconscious – and he had looked dreadfully limp – he wouldn't be needing his sunglasses right away.

Maybe he only wore them out of doors.

I'll ask Mother to see that he gets them, Grig decided. She'll be able to find out which hospital he was taken to, and make sure that the glasses are taken to him. Mother was fine at things like that, she always knew what must be done, and who was the best person to do it. She understood what was important. And – Grig thought – the glasses must be *very* important to Professor Bercy, or he would hardly have risked his life in the traffic to try and recover them. Could they be his only pair? Surely not. If he was such an important scientist, you'd think he'd have dozens of pairs.

The glasses were now in Grig's anorak pocket, safely cradled in his left hand; the right hand was still in the iron grip of Anna, who was hauling him along as if the Deluge had begun and they were the last two passengers for the Ark.

Eugène was there before them, waiting in the usual room; but, surprisingly, he didn't seem annoyed at their lateness, just listened to Anna's breathless explanation with his wide frog-smile, said it was quite a little excitement they'd had, and did the man bleed a lot? Then, even more surprisingly, he produced a small pâtissier's cardboard carton, tied with shiny paper string, and said to Grig, 'Here, mon mouton, this is for you. For your petit manger. A cake.'

Grig generally brought an apple to the Louvre. Indeed he had one today, in his right-hand pocket. Eugène called the apple Grig's petit manger. While Anna and Eugène sat and talked, Grig was in the habit of eating his apple slowly and inconspicuously, as he walked about looking at the pictures.

'Go on,' repeated Eugène. 'The cake's for you.'

Grig did not want to appear rude or doubtful or suspicious

at this unexpected gift; but just the same he *was* suspicious. Eugène had never before showed any friendly feelings; the things he said to Grig were generally sharp or spiteful or teasing; why, today, should he have brought this piece of pâtisserie – rather expensive it looked, too, done up so carefully with a gold name on the side of the box? Eugène was always shabby, in worn jeans and a rubbed black leather jacket, and his sneakers looked as if they let in the water; why should he suddenly bring out such an offering?

'Say thank you!' snapped Anna. 'It's very kind of Eugène to have brought you a cake!'

'Thank you,' said Grig. He added doubtfully, 'But I don't think people are allowed to eat in here.'

'Oh, don't be silly. Who's going to see? Anyway, you always eat your apple – here, I'll undo the string.'

It was tied in a hopelessly tight, hard knot Anna nibbled through it with her strong white teeth, and Eugène made some low-voiced remark in French too quick for Grig to catch, which made her flush and laugh, though she looked rather cross. Once the string was undone, the little waxed box opened out like a lily to disclose a gooey glistening brown cake in a fluted paper cup.

'Aren't you lucky; it's a rum baba,' said Anna.

As it happened, a rum baba was Grig's least favourite kind of cake: too syrupy, too squashy, too scented. He wasn't greatly surprised, or disappointed; he would have expected Eugène to have a nasty taste in cakes, or anything else. He thanked

Eugène again with great politeness, then strolled away from the pair at a slow, casual pace, looking at the pictures on the walls as he went.

'Eat that up fast, now, or it'll drip syrup all over everywhere,' Anna called after him sharply; and then she began talking to Eugène, telling him some long story, gabbling it out, while he listened without seeming to take in much of what she said, his eyes roving after Grig, who wandered gently into the next room, and then into the one after that, wondering, as he went, if it would be possible to slip the pastry into a little bin without being noticed.

'Don't go too far now—' He could hear Anna's voice, fainter in the distance behind him.

As usual, there weren't any other people in the suite of small dark rooms. Grig supposed that the pictures here were not thought to be very important; though some of them were his particular favourites.

There was one of an astronomer with a globe; Grig always liked to look at that; and another of a woman making lace on a pillow; she wore a yellow dress, and had a contented, absorbed expression that reminded Grig of his mother while she was working on her embroidery. There was a picture that he liked of a bowl and a silver mug, with some apples; and another of a china jug with bunches of grapes and a cut-up pomegranate that he deeply admired. Grig intended to be a painter himself by and by; he always stood before this picture for a long, long time, wondering how many years it took to learn to paint grapes like that, so that you could actually see the bloom on them, and the shine on the pearl handle of the knife, and the glisten on the red seeds of the pomegranate. Then there was a picture of a boy about Grig's age, sitting at a desk, playing with a spinning top. The boy was really a bit old to be playing with a childish toy such as a top; you could see that he had just come across it, maybe among some forgotten things at the back of his desk, and had taken it out to give it a spin because he was bored and had nothing better to do just then; he was watching it thoughtfully, consideringly; in fact he had the same intent expression as that on the face of the woman working at the lace on her pillow. Perhaps, thought Grig, that boy grew up to be some kind of scientist or mathematician (he must have lived long ago, for his clothes were old fashioned, a satin jacket) and at the sight of the top spinning, some interesting idea about speed or circles or patterns or time had come into his head. The boy with the top was one of Grig's favourite pictures, and he always stood in front of it for quite a while.

Then he was about to move on to his very favourite of all, when his attention was caught by an old lady who had been walking through the rooms in the contrary direction. She paused beside Grig and glanced out through the window into the big central courtyard. What she saw there seemed to surprise her very much and arouse her disapproval too. She let out several exclamations – 'Oh, la la! Tiens! Quel horreur!' – put on a pair of long-distance glasses to take a better look at what was going on outside, stared frowningly for a moment or two more, then muttered some grumbling comment to herself, in which Grig caught several references to Napoleon III; then, shaking her head in a condemning manner, she went stomping on her way. After waiting until she was out of sight, Grig put a knee on the leather window seat and hoisted himself up to look out, in order to see what was happening outside that aroused such feelings of outrage in the old girl.

What he saw in the quadrangle made him surprised that he had not noticed it as they made their way in; but he remembered that then he had been looking back for the ambulance, and worrying about Professor Bercy's glasses, that must have been why he did not take in the oddness of the scene.

A wooden palisade had been built around the central part of the quadrangle, and it seemed that digging was going on inside this fence, a big excavator with grabbing jaw could be seen swinging its head back and forth, dumping soil and rubble in a truck that stood by the paling.

Then, outside the barrier – and this was probably what had shocked the old lady – three full-sized chestnut trees lay, crated up, on huge towing trucks, the sort that usually carry heavy machinery or sardine-like batches of new cars. The trees all had their leaves on, and their roots too; the roots had been carefully bundled up in great cylindrical containers made from wooden slats – like flower tubs, only a million times bigger, Grig thought. It appeared that the trees had been dug up from the central area and were being taken away, perhaps to be replanted somewhere else, just like geraniums or begonias in the public gardens. What on earth could Napoleon III have to do with it? Grig wondered, thinking of the old lady. Had he planted the trees, perhaps? They looked as if they could easily be over a hundred years old. Napoleon III had done a lot to beautify Paris, Grig knew. Perhaps among the roots of the trees, now parcelled up like bean sprouts, there might be coins, francs and centimes from 1850, or medals or jewels, or all kinds of other relics. I'd love to have a closer look at them, thought Grig, and, his left hand happening to touch Professor Bercy's sun-glasses in his anorak pocket, at the moment when this thought came to him, he absentmindedly pulled out the glasses and perched them on his nose.

They fitted him quite well. He could feel that the earpieces were made of some light, strong, springy material that clung, of its own accord, not uncomfortably, to the sides of his head. The lenses, squarish in shape, were very large; in fact they almost entirely covered his face, so that he could see nothing except through their slightly pinkish screen. For a moment they misted over, after he had put them on; then they began to clear, and he looked through them, out of the window and into the courtyard.

For years and years and years afterwards, Grig went over and over that scene in his memory, trying to recall every last detail of it. When he had grown up and become a painter, he painted it many times – the whole scene, or bits of it, small fragments, differing figures from it – over and over and over again. 'Ah, that's a Rainborrow,' people would say, walking into a gallery, from thirty, forty feet away, 'you can always tell a Rainborrow.'

What did he see? He would have found it almost impossible to give a description in words. *Layers*, he thought. It's like seeing all the layers together. Different levels. People now – and people *then*. People when? People right back. How many thousands of years people must have been doing things on this bit of ground, so close to the River Seine. And, there they all are!

As well as the people *then*, he could see the people *now*; several students, a boy riding a bicycle, a policeman, and the three great chestnut trees, tied on their trucks like invalids on stretchers. And, sure enough, in among the roots of the trees, Grig could catch a glimpse of all kinds of objects, knobby and dusty, solid and sparkling; perhaps that was what Professor Bercy had been coming to look at? The glasses must have had a fairly strong magnifying power, as well as this other mysterious ability they had to show the layers of time lying one behind another.

What else could they show?

Grig turned carefully, for he felt a little dizzy, to look inwards at the room behind him. The first thing that caught his gaze, as he turned, was Eugène's gift, the rum baba, which he still clutched awkwardly in his right hand. Through Professor Bercy's pink-tinted glasses the cake looked even nastier than it had when seen by the naked eye. It was darker in colour – dark blood-brown, oozy and horrible; embedded in the middle of it he now saw two pills, one pink, one yellow. The pills hadn't been visible before, but through the pink lenses Grig could see them quite distinctly: sunk in the wet mass of dough they were becoming a bit mushy at the edges, beginning to wilt into the surrounding cake.

Why should Eugène want to give him cake with pills in it? What in the world was he up to? With a jerk of disgust, Grig dropped the little pâtissérie box on the floor. Nobody else was in the room. With his heel, he slid box and cake out of view under the window seat, then wiped his fingers – the syrup had already started to ooze through the carton – wiped his fingers vigorously, again and again, on a tissue. He glanced behind him to make sure that his action had not been seen by Anna or Eugène – but no, thank goodness, they were still safely out of sight, several rooms away.

Turning in the opposite direction, Grig walked quickly on into the next room, where his favourite picture of all hung.

This was a painting of a horse, by an artist called Potter. Grig always thought of it as Potter's Grey. The picture was not at all large: perhaps one foot by eighteen inches, if as much; and the horse was not particularly handsome, rather the contrary. It was a grey, with some blobby dark dappled spots. Grig could hardly have said why he liked it so much. He was sure that the painter must have been very fond of the horse. Perhaps it belonged to him. Perhaps he called it Grey, and always gave it an apple or a carrot before sitting down with his easel and his tubes or pots of paint. The picture was over three hundred years old; a label said that Potter had been a Dutchman who lived from 1625 to 1654. He was only twenty-nine when he died, not old. Mother, who knew all sorts of odd things, once told Grig that Potter died of tuberculosis; which could have been cured these days. Grig thought that very sad. If Potter had lived now, he could have painted many more pictures of horses, instead of having his life cut off in the middle.

Anyway, this Grey was as good a horse as you could wish to meet, and, on each visit to the Louvre, Grig always walked to where his portrait hung, on the left of the doorway, between door and window, and – after first checking to make certain no one else was in the room – stood staring until his whole mind was filled with pleasure, with the whole essence of the horse; then he would pull the apple out of his pocket, take a bite of it himself, hold the rest up on the palm of his hand as you should when feeding a horse, and say, 'Have a bite, Grey.'

He did so now. But this time, something happened that had never happened before.

Grey put a gentle, silvery muzzle with soft nostrils sprouting white hairs out of the picture *and took the apple from Grig's hand.*

Then he withdrew his head into the frame and ate the apple with evident satisfaction.

Grig gasped. He couldn't help it – he was so pleased that he felt warm tears spring into his eyes. Blinking them away, he looked rapidly round the small gallery – and saw, without any particular surprise, that every picture was alive, living its life in its own way as it must have done when the artist painted it: a fly was buzzing over the grapes that lay beside the china jug, some men were hauling down the sail of a ship, the woman, winding the bobbins of her lace-pillow, carefully finished off one and began another. Then she looked up and gave Grig an absent-minded smile.

There were other people in the room too, outside the pictures, walking about – people in all kinds of different clothes. Grig wished, from the bottom of his heart, that he could hear what they were saying, wished he could speak to them and ask questions – but Professor Bercy's glasses were only for seeing, they couldn't help him to hear. You'd want headphones too, Grig thought, straining his ears nonetheless to try and catch the swish of a dress, the crunch of Grey finishing the apple – but all he heard was the angry note of Anna's voice, 'Grig! Where in the *world* have you *got* to?' and the clack of her wooden-soled shoes on the polished gallery floor as she came hurrying in search of him. Grig couldn't resist glancing back at Potter's horse – but the apple was all finished, not a sign of it remained – then he felt Anna's fingers close on his wrist like pincers, and she was hurrying him towards the exit, angrily gabbling into his ear, 'What in heaven's name have you been *doing* with yourself all this time? Can't you see it's started to rain and we'll be late, we'll have to take a taxi—'

All this time she was hurrying Grig through one gallery after another, and Eugène was walking beside them, looking a little amused and calmly indifferent to Anna's scolding of her charge.

115

Grig himself was still dizzy, shaken, confused and distracted. Firstly, he would have liked to stop and stare with minute attention at each of the huge canvases they were now passing in the main galleries. Because – just *look* at what was happening in that coronation scene with Emperor Napoleon putting the crown on his queen's head, and the Pope behind him – and those people struggling to keep on the raft which was heaving about among huge waves, though some of them were dead, you could see – and the lady lying twiddling her fingers on a sofa – and the man on a horse – they were all alive; it was like looking through a series of windows at what was going on beyond the glass.

But also, Grig was absolutely horrified at what he saw when he looked across Anna at Eugène; the sight of Eugène's face was so extremely frightening that Grig's eyes instantly flicked away from it each time; but then he felt compelled to look back in order to convince himself of what he had seen.

All the *workings* were visible: inside the skull the brain, inside the brain, memory, feelings, hopes and plans. The memories were all dreadful ones, the hopes and plans were all wicked. It was like, from the height of a satellite, watching a great storm rage across a whole continent; you could see the whirl of cloud, the flash of lightning, you could guess at uprooted trees, flooded rivers and smashed buildings. You could see that Eugène planned to do an enormous amount of damage; and it was plain that, here and now, he hated Grig and had a plan about him; what kind of a plan Grig didn't exactly know, but little details of it that came to him in flashes made him shudder.

'Come on, hurry up,' said Anna, buttoning her raincoat, when they reached the entrance lobby. 'Button your jacket, put your scarf round. Eugène's getting a taxi, and he'll drop us at the Embassy and go on—'

'*No!*' said Grig. He didn't intend going with Eugène in any taxi. And he knew well that Eugène had no plans at all to drop them at the Embassy.

'What do you mean, *no*?' said Anna furiously. 'What in the world are you *talking* about? Don't act like a baby. You'll do as I say, or else—'

'*No*,' repeated Grig doggedly, and yanked at the wrist which she still grasped in an unshakeable grip. He looked at Anna and saw that she was not wicked like Eugène, but stupid all through, solid like a block of marble or plaster. It would be useless to argue with her and say, 'Eugène is bad. He has some awful plan. Why did he put pills in that cake?'

Grig was still terribly confused and distracted by the complicated sights, the layers and layers of different happenings that were taking place all around him. But at last he realized what he must do. With his free hand he pulled the pink-tinted glasses off his face, and said, 'Please, Anna. Put these on for a moment. Look at Eugène, when he comes in—'

'Oh, don't be so *silly*! Why in the world should I? Where ever did you *get* those glasses?' She had forgotten all about the accident, and Professor Bercy. 'What is this, anyway, some kind of silly joke?'

'Please put them on, Anna. If you don't—' What could he do, what could he possibly do? Then, with a gulp of relief, he remembered some practical advice that his mother had once given him. 'It sounds babyish,' she had said, 'but if ever you are in a tight corner, *yell*. It attracts attention, people will come running, that will give you time to think; so never mind that you may feel a fool, just do it, just yell.'

'If you don't put them on,' said Grig, ' I shall scream so loud that people will think I've gone mad. I mean it, Anna.'

'I think you already *have* gone mad,' she said, but she looked at him, saw that he did mean it, and put on the glasses. At that moment Eugène came back through the glass entrance door, his black leather jacket shiny with rain, and on his face a big false smile. Without the glasses, Grig could no longer see the evil workings of Eugène's brain – which was in every way a relief – but just the same, he knew exactly how false that smile was.

'OK,' said Eugène, 'venez vite, tous les deux—' and then Anna, looking at him, started to scream. Her scream was far, far louder than any yell that Grig could have raised, he had no need even to open his mouth. The smile dropped from Eugène's face like paper off a wet window; he stared at Anna first with shock, then with rage. '*Come* on, girl, what *is* this?' he said, trying to grab her hand, but she twisted away from him, still shrieking like a machine that has blown off its safety-valve. 'No – no – no – get away – get away – you're *horrible*—'

By this time, as Mother had prophesied, people were running towards them, people were staring and exclaiming and pushing close, trying to discover what was the matter with Anna. Now Eugène's nerve suddenly broke. He let out a couple of wicked, hissing swearwords, turned on his heel, was out of the glass doors, and vanished from view. At the same moment Anna, furiously dragging the tinted glasses from her face, flung them on the stone floor as if they were poisoned, trampled them into fragments, and burst into hysterical sobs.

'Would you please telephone my father?' Grig said to a uniformed woman who seemed like someone in a position of authority. 'I think my gouvernante has been taken ill. My father is the British Ambassador,' and he gave her the Embassy number.

So they went home in a taxi after all.

'Please can you take me to see Professor Bercy in hospital?' Grig asked his mother next day, when Anna was under sedatives and the care of a doctor, and a new au pair girl was being advertised for, and in the meantime Lady Julia Rainborrow was leaving her ambassadorial duties to take her son for an airing.

But she said, 'Darling, no; I'm afraid I can't. It was on the news this morning. He died last night in hospital; he never recovered consciousness.'

'Oh,' said Grig. 'Oh.'

He had dreaded having to tell Professor Bercy that his glasses had been smashed; but this was far worse.

I wonder if they *were* his only pair? Grig thought, plodding along the street beside Lady Julia. Or if other people – the other scientists who worked with him – knew about them too?

'Where would you like to go?' Grig's mother asked him. 'It's not a very nice day – I'm afraid it looks like rain again.'

'Can we go to the Louvre?'

'Are you sure you want to go there?' she said doubtfully.

'Yes, I would like to,' said Grig, and so they walked in the direction of the Louvre, finding it hard to talk to one another, Grig very unhappy about Professor Bercy, dead before he had finished his life-work – and what a work! – while Lady Julia worried about Grig. But what can you do? You can't look after somebody twenty-four hours a day. Ambassadors' sons have to take their chance, like everybody else.

Going quickly through the suit of dark little galleries, Grig came to the picture of Potter's Grey. He stood and stared at the dappled horse, very lovingly, very intently, and thought: Yesterday I gave you an apple, and you put out your head and took it from my hand, and I stroked your nose. I shall come back tomorrow, and next week, and the week after, and that will never, never happen again. But it *did* happen, and I remember it.

Do you remember it, Grey?

He thought that the grey horse looked at him very kindly.

Ash Talks
to
Bone

The ghost of a cuckoo
in a skeleton tree
called a promise
to the ghost of me –

a ghostly cuckoo
in a skeleton larch
in doubtful April
or spectral March

take heart, take heart
called the ghostly bird
(or this is what
I thought I heard)

you and I
are ash and bone
you and I
are dead and gone

but seeds are waiting
under all
trees will grow again
strong and tall

deep in the future
centuries past
nuclear night
will end at last

dawn will break
and life rejoice
in unknown words
and a foreign voice

take heart, take heart
called the ghostly bird
(or this was what
I thought I heard)

Crusader's Toby

SAND WAS WHAT the Knights came for, and sand there was, plenty of it. North of Swaycliffe the dunes stretched away, acres and acres of them, like the sandy breakers of an inland sea, crested with shaggy tufts of grass – long, swooping curves of sand, over which the gulls and curlews flew in parallel swoops as if they were playing on a switchback of air.

'There's enough sand here to bury the Pyramids,' Toby Knight said once, and his father said, 'You might as well throw in the Taj Mahal and the Empire State Building while you're at it.'

In between the dunes and the North Sea lay the beach itself, flat, white, empty sand, as empty and shining as the moon.

The curious thing was that neither of Toby's parents actually made much use of the sand.

To the right of the village – which was only eight houses, a Post Office, and a pub – the little Sway river ran out, noiselessly fast, clear as pale brown ink in its sandy channel, pouring down past the huge width of the beach, into the waiting sea. And here, day-long every day, Mr Knight stood fishing on a comma-shaped spit of sand, around which the silent hurrying river had to curl its way. Sometimes he caught trout, sometimes he caught sea-fish, sometimes he caught nothing at all, but there he stayed, like a motionless speck in the vast bright emptiness of the beach.

And Toby's mother, meanwhile, was busy writing a book. She took her portable typewriter every day and climbed up to the little ruined church on the cliff, and wrote there.

The cliff was actually a grassy headland across on the other side of the Sway river; Mrs Knight had to walk a quarter of a mile inland up the river-bank and go over the bridge, and up a steep sandy path to reach it. Mostly Toby went with her and carried her typewriter. He liked to pay a daily visit to the crusader in the church. While his mother settled herself in the sun, leaning against a bit of flying-buttress, sitting on one chunk of Norman masonry and with her typewriter balanced on another, Toby went inside the airy roofless shell of sea-whitened stone to visit Sir Bertrand de Swaye, who lay gazing calmly towards the east, with his legs crossed and his hand on the hilt of his sword. He looked comfortable enough, except that his feet were tipped up higher than his head because the ground underneath his tomb had subsided. In fact the whole church was falling into the sea, piece by piece; Sir Bertrand's wife and five children had already disappeared into the sea several years before.

'Isn't the church rather a dangerous place for Mum to go and do her writing?' Toby asked his father once, but Mr Knight said no. 'It's only in the winter that the storms are bad enough to loosen the cliff and make bits of it slide into the sea. Anyway I did make her promise to sit at the landward end of the church. If she sits there I can see her when I'm fishing and we can wave to one another.'

The church certainly still looked solid enough, with its round arches all decorated in zigzag dogtooth, like the ends of crackers, and its eight massive circular pillars holding up nothing but sky.

The following spring, though, when they came back, two of the pillars had gone, fallen into the sea, and Sir Bertrand was tipped even more head down, though he still appeared quite at ease, gazing towards Jerusalem, with his hand on his sword.

The best thing about Sir Bertrand, of course, was his dog, who, curiously enough, was also named Toby. This Toby was not at all like the usual crusaders' dogs who lie looking rather meek and suppressed under their masters' feet; he was too big for that, to start with. He lay on a kind of step at the end of Sir Bertrand's tomb, lower than his master, but with his head raised vigilantly high so that Sir Bertrand, looking past his own armoured toes, could probably just see Toby's upraised muzzle.

Old Mr Brooman, who lived in the village, said that Toby might be a kind of Afghan hound. 'Well, he could ha' been, stands to reason. Sir Bertrand got him when he was out in the Holy Land, they say. It's all overland from there to Afghanistan. The Arabs and Persians had Salukis; it's common sense that they must all ha' been related once.'

Mr Brooman lived in a little cobble-built cottage at the end of the short village street, right by the beach. He was retired, his wife dead, his children long since scattered about the world; one son was in South Africa, a daughter in New Zealand. He knew a lot about dogs; that was how Toby first met him, during their first summer at Swaycliffe, when Harriet, Toby's Jack Russell terrier, developed a bad limp and was very sorry for herself. There was no vet in the village, but someone suggested that Mr Brooman might be able to help. And so he had: he was so very kind to Harriet, carefully examining her foot, finding the splinter that was the cause of the trouble, soaking it out, disinfecting the wound and putting on it some ointment of his own invention which healed it overnight, that Harriet instantly fell in love with him. After that, each time they came back to Swaycliffe, the very first thing she did was to gallop along to Mr Brooman's house, throw herself down in front of him and roll over and over, waving her paws in the air.

Mr Brooman had had various dogs in the past. His last one had been an Alsatian called Minnie. When Minnie died, he told Toby, he had resolved to have no more dogs. 'She was the finish. I knew I could never love any dog better than Minnie, so it was best not to have another. Besides, I'm getting on myself; I wouldn't like for to die and leave a dog lonely. No, that wouldn't do. A human being's got distractions; if someone dies, or goes off and leaves you lonely, there's things you can do to cheer yourself: you can read, you can study, you can do carpentry. But a dog can't do any of those things.'

Mr Brooman did a lot of carpentry; one summer he made a vaulting-horse for Toby so that he could practise athletics out on the empty beach; and he made a strong little table for Toby's mother and carried it up to the church for her, so that she could type more comfortably.

' 'Tis all made from bits of ship's teak, washed up on the sands, so that'll take no harm from the weather, ma'am; you can just leave it up there, rain or shine.'

Mr Brooman himself visited the church almost every evening; he had done for years; it was he who had given the crusader's dog the name Toby.

'I always did think it suited him, some'ow. Funny you should have the same name, my boy. That's what's known as a coincidence. Yes, I've bin a-visiting this 'ere old Toby for donkey's years; him an' me's had many a gossip. Wonderful bit of carving that is, when you think what a long time he's been here. Seven 'undred years old, that dog is.'

Crusader's Toby was a big dog, tall and rangy like a greyhound, but stronger-looking. His coat was smooth but wavy, and his ears, cocked high and intelligently, were fringed inside like the petals of a chrysanthemum. As for his tail, one could see that it had been tremendously plumed, with long swags hanging below it all the way from tip to base, like the underside of an ostrich feather. Some of the plumes had broken off or worn away, unfortunately, but there were still enough left to show. He had a long, keen intelligent nose, big eyes well set in a broad forehead, and big strong feet.

'Good for running in all that sand,' Mr Brooman said. 'Wonderful clever those crusaders' dogs were – they could sniff out a Turk from a Christian, it's said.'

There were several legends about Crusader's Toby: he had saved his master's life three times over, once in battle against the Saracens, once from assassins sent by the Old Man of the Mountains to way-

lay him on the way back from the Holy Land, and once within sight of home when his ship was wrecked off the mouth of the Sway, and Toby had swum through the dangerous undertow, supporting his wounded master's head on his own powerful shoulders.

'That was why Sir Bertrand wanted his memorial carved separate, because he set such store by the dog, and he had it done while he was still alive, to make sure it was done proper. In fact, there's some as say Sir Bertrand carved it hisself. He was a clever man. He writ a little book, too, all in Latin, about his adventures on the crusades, and it's still in the museum in York. That came out o' the castle that was here once; it was a Norman castle, up there on the headland by the church. But that fell into the sea two 'undred year back.'

Toby resolved to go and see Sir Bertrand's book in the museum one day, but York was a long way off. 'It's a pity it couldn't be kept here in the village,' he said.

'Ah, it is,' said old Mr Brooman. 'I don't hold wi' taking things away from where they belong. Things what comes from the village ought to stay in the village.'

Mr Brooman was a native of Swaycliffe, born and bred, though it was true he had travelled a long way from home in his time.

'In the army I was, see; had to go where I was sent. I been in India and in Australia too; and in the Mediterranean. Gibraltar, and then Malta; lots o' crusaders' stuff there. And in Hong Kong I was, for a while.'

Mr Brooman had also, when he was young, been a long-distance runner. It was hard to imagine this now; he was bent and red-faced, with broken veins in his cheeks, and a ragged white moustache; the front part of his head was bald, a thin fringe of white hair curved round the back. And he was very lame indeed with rheumatism and arthritis, never walked without the help of his thick stick. But while he was still in the army he had been an Olympic runner, had carried a blazing torch in the relay from Athens up across Europe in 1936, and had won a gold medal, which he kept on his mantelshelf alongside Minnie's photograph.

During the Easter holidays, when Toby was running and racing out on the sands with Harriet, who went wild with joy every time she saw the great shining bare flatness of the beach, Mr Brooman would often come limping out and sit on the cobbled sea-wall and shout advice.

'Don't clench your fists up so and tighten your chest, boy! You want to run easy, like as if your whole body was in one piece; you don't want to waste any little bit of energy on anything but the running itself, see? Mind you,' he added kindly, 'you shape well;

you'll be a sprinter, I can see that; I'd fancy you at a hundred yards.'

And in the summer, when Toby came back and said that he had won the junior hundred yards at school, Mr Brooman said, 'Well there. What did I tell you?' That was the summer Mr Brooman made the vaulting-horse, and spent long days out on the sand, teaching Toby to do long-fly and short-fly and something called high-and-over.

In the evenings they went for walks along the beach, north or south; Mr Brooman limping lopsidedly but rapidly along, Toby hunting for shells and beach treasures, Harriet racing backwards and forwards across their track, now up on the dunes, now right down at the edge of the sea, which, when the tide was out, seemed about a mile away. The sun sinking behind the land dyed the crests of the dunes all red and ragged; and when it was down out of sight there would be a spreading luminous pink afterglow, turning the whole sky a brilliant peach-colour. It was possible to walk north along the coast for five miles before you came to the next town, Calnmouth, but Toby and Mr Brooman didn't often get as far as that, because, after the sun went down, dusk fell quickly, and then Mr Brooman would say that his leg was getting tired.

At Easter, when they came back after a winter's absence, Toby noticed that the familiar dunes had completely changed their shape: mountains had piled up where he remembered valleys; a favourite little hidden dell of his, where he had been accustomed to go and read on long hot peaceful afternoons, was now a wide-open shell-backed plateau with a strange twisted tree, smooth and grey from long soaking in the sea, half-buried in the middle of it.

'Ah, it was a terrible winter for storms,' said old Mr Brooman –

who had not changed at all since last year. 'Sometimes the wind blew for ten-fifteen days at a stretch; all the coast's changed along here an' there's a great bit out o' the beach up Calnmouth way and they've had to build a plank bridge across. You'll find changes up at the church, too.'

Toby saw what Mr Brooman meant as soon as he had run across the bridge and up the cliff path: two more of the round columns had fallen, and were to be seen, in bits, down below on the beach, half-buried in sand. Sadder still, Sir Bertrand de Swaye had disappeared too; only Toby remained, still with his head raised, gazing alertly towards the distant east, as if he wondered where his master had gone.

Poor Toby, thought the human Toby, remembering what Mr Brooman had said: 'I wouldn't like for to die and leave a dog lonely.' It seemed hard that he should have lost his master after they had been so long together.

That evening, when they went for their first walk along the wet beach, pink with sunset reflections, Mr Brooman told Toby a queer thing.

Harriet, mad with happiness at so much space after her confinement in London all winter long, was racing in crazy circles, down to the sea, up to the dunes, tearing back to Toby to spatter him with sand, then off again into the far distance to tease a feeding flock of gulls or sandpipers, dashing with a volley of barks among them to drive them into the air.

'Now, you watch, quiet-like,' said Mr Brooman. 'I don't *know* as it'll work, for I've never done it when there was someone else along, but watch and see.'

He pulled out his dog-whistle. This was a small silver gadget which he had often shown Toby. You could blow it like an ordinary whistle, but you could also twist the mouthpiece around, so that the sound it produced was too high for human ears, and could be heard by dogs alone.

They were walking on the beach south of the Sway river mouth, below the headland; one or two bits of broken Norman column lay near the cliff. Toby had already searched all over the sands for Sir Bertrand himself and had found no sign of him; the winter seas must have broken him up, or the undertow had dragged him out and buried him deep.

Above, on the grassy height, the frail bonelike ruins of the church were outlined in black against a pale-pink sky.

'Now then,' said Mr Brooman, and blew his silent whistle.

Harriet heard it at once.

She came racing towards them from far away on the sea's edge as if she had been pulled back on the end of a long elastic string.

But then, when she had nearly returned to Mr Brooman and Toby, she began behaving in an odd and unexpected manner. Instead of dashing up against them and covering them with sand in her usual way, she began barking and bouncing about, crouching right down on her elbows and then shooting up in the air, twisting sideways, sometimes rolling over and over, somersaulting and panting, with yards of her tongue out of her mouth as if she were laughing.

'How queer! She looks just as if she's playing with another dog – that's the way she carries on with some of her friends in London,' Toby said, puzzled.

'Ah. That's it,' said Mr Brooman. He put the whistle back in his pocket.

Now Harriet was off again, on a long slant back to the sea. But she ran with her head cocked to the left, taking sudden sideways swerves and snatches, as if another dog ran beside her and she was playfully bumping up against him, butting him with her head or shoulder, taking a teasing nip out of his ear.

'It's *crazy*,' said Toby. 'Mr Brooman – do you think—?'

What he wanted to suggest seemed so ridiculous that he hesitated, but Mr Brooman said it for him.

'Toby from up above's come down for a run and she's a-playing with him.'

'But—'

'He wakes up, now, you see, when I blows the old whistle. He'll be glad to have company. There's no dogs in the village since Mrs Grimes at the Post Office lost her Blackie. Old Toby likes a bit of company, you can see that.'

'But why,' said Toby the boy, watching Harriet, who looked as if she were being rolled over and over by a large invisible paw, 'why didn't he ever come down before?'

'Well, he didn't need to, did he? He had his master alongside. So long as they was together he was pleased to stay there. But now it's different. He's hunting for his master, see? Times I've been out with him, on the shore, I've felt him running along, by the water's edge, a-looking and a-looking to see if he can't make out where has his master got to. Sometimes,' said Mr Brooman, looking around the huge empty beach to make sure no one could hear what he was going to say, 'sometimes I've almost been sure I could see his footprints by the edges of the water where the sand's all wet and soft – or the splashes he was a-throwing up when he went in the sea. And then he'll come along close arter me, I can almost hear him, pad, pad, right be'ind, and I can hear him thinking, You're a yuman, why can't you tell me where he is?'

Toby looked at Mr Brooman with some doubt. Could the old man be getting a bit cracked from living alone?

But then Harriet came trotting up, tired for the moment, covered with sand, ready to fall in alongside the humans and go at their pace. She had no attention to spare for them, though; she was engrossed in conversation with someone bigger and taller and invisible who was lolloping at an easy pace beside her.

'*Do* dogs have ghosts?' Toby said.

Mr Brooman thought for a while.

'The way I figure it is this,' he said finally. 'What is there in you that lasts? It's your soul, ennit? Call it that. The body part of you dries out and turns into earth, even the bones do that, give 'em long enough, arter you die. But there's some bit of you that's different, that makes you different from any other person, that sends invisible streamers out like a jellyfish, and they hooks on to things round about you while you're still alive. Call that your soul. And that'll still be there after you've died, hooked on to all those things round about you that you was fond of while you was alive. See what I mean?'

'You think dogs do that too?'

'Why not? Special if a dog gets to be very fond of his master. Then they hook together, like. I tell you what I think,' said Mr

Brooman, glancing back at the black shell of the roofless church silhouetted against the pink sky on the headland behind them. 'I think that Sir Bertrand did carve that there statue of Toby hisself. It must ha' taken him a long, long time, it was done so faithful. And while he was a-doing it, a bit of Toby's soul must ha' got knitted into the stone, like, an' it's still there. Arter all, they say that painters put their soul into their pictures, don't they? You put your soul into anything you're really keen on.'

'Well then,' said Toby, 'is it Toby's soul, or Sir Bertrand's?'

'Now you foxed me there,' said Mr Brooman. 'Tell you the truth, I don't rightly know. Maybe it's both. Maybe when you get a friendship like that, they gets kind of woven together.'

Toby glanced again to his right, at Harriet so happy with her new friend. Having got her breath, she was beginning to bounce and gambol again, and next moment she set off on another half-mile sprint, down to the edge of the sea, and into the water, which as a rule she was reluctant to enter unless somebody went with her.

Were there two sets of splashes or only one?

That night when they got back to the house Harriet flung herself down on the hearth-rug and slept like a worn-out dog, not even stirring and twitching with dreams as she usually did. And the moment she woke next morning she dashed outside, looking alertly about as if she expected somebody; she seemed rather puzzled and crestfallen at the emptiness of the salty, sunny village street.

'I suppose you'll have to wait till this evening, Harriet,' Toby told her. 'Till Mr Brooman blows his whistle. But we can go up to the church and have a look at old stone Toby, if you like.'

They walked up to the church with Mrs Knight when she went to do her daily chapter. There lay stone Toby, basking in the April sunshine, but Harriet was not interested in him. The Toby she expected must be somewhere locked inside the stone, or else already down below searching for his master on the sun-swept, wind-swept beach.

Just in case he was somewhere inside, Toby sat down for a moment with his arm round stone Toby's neck, and murmured into the fringed clever uplifted ear:

'Good boy then, good old boy! Don't you worry, Toby, I'm sure he's waiting for you, down there in the sea. And Lady Swaye and the children will be there too. You'll have to learn to be a water-dog, Toby.'

Motionless, apparently deaf to this consolation, stone Toby went on gazing vigilantly towards the east. But Harriet, jealous and impatient, barked and pranced from side to side, and tugged at her master's sleeve until he got up and followed her down the steep and slithery sand path which led on over the headland and back to the beach. Ghost-Toby did not join them there; it seemed that wherever he was, he would only come out to play when summoned by Mr Brooman's whistle. But that never failed. Dusk after dusk the four of them went along at their varying paces over the wet sand, live dog and ghost-dog racing ahead, Mr Brooman limping, helped by his stick, telling stories of Malta and Gibraltar, of the dogs of Hong Kong and the plains of Yugoslavia where he had carried the Olympic torch, while Toby the boy listened and watched Harriet's antics, and sometimes raced ahead, alongside of her and her unseen companion, practising for the four hundred and forty yards, which was his next ambition.

When the Knights came back in the summer, Toby with a silver cup to show off proudly to Mr Brooman, stone Toby was still up there on the headland. And as in the spring, he joined them invisibly on their walks in the long twilit evenings.

'Sometimes, nowadays,' confided Mr Brooman, 'he'll come right along the village street, right up to the 'ouse with me. But I never yet got him to come inside. 'E always stops outside the door.'

It was a happy summer. The long salty sunlit days stretched in a peaceful shining chain, one after another, each exactly like the one before, and yet all as different as the shells on the beach; time seemed to have slowed down. Toby's father fished, and his mother wrote, and stone Toby drowsed in the sun all day, up on his headland, waiting for Sir Bertrand, and came down in the evenings to race and play.

'Well, well,' said Mr Brooman rather sadly when September came, and it was time for the Knights to leave, 'I'll miss you, young Toby, and Harriet, when the nights draw in and the winds get a-blowing. It seems a long time to spring. I'm not getting any younger, and that's the truth.'

Looking carefully at Mr Brooman, Toby saw that it was the truth. Somehow, unnoticed by him, the old man seemed to have shrunk in the course of the summer; the skin hung more loosely on his face, and his limp was more pronounced.

'It's good that you've got Crusader's Toby to keep you company. Maybe when it gets to be real winter you'll be able to persuade him into your house.'

'Ah; maybe I will,' said Mr Brooman thoughtfully, and Toby

felt a sudden queer pang of anxiety – was it for the old man or for stone Toby up there on his headland? Would they be able to look after each other through the storms of the coming winter?

'I'll try and get Mum and Dad to come down at Christmas,' he said. 'I've often asked them and Dad did promise that some year we might.'

'Ah, you do that! Swaycliffe's grand in winter, when the sea piles up and roars for days on end, and the sky gets black as ink and the beach is all white with snow. It's worth seeing, that is.'

By hard pleading, Toby did manage to convince his parents that they should come back to Swaycliffe in the winter holidays. All the time they were packing the car with food and warm clothes and extra bedding, Toby was on edge with expectation. During the drive down on Christmas Eve he longed for the sigh and smell of the sea, all winter-wild, and for the company of Mr Brooman and Crusader's Toby. A gale had been lashing the North Sea coast all the week before Christmas. Would Toby be all right? Would he still be there, up in the church?

As soon as they had arrived and unpacked the car, Toby ran along the snowy lane to Mr Brooman's. But the house was dark, shut and locked. Full of worry, he went on to the Post Office to ask Mrs Grimes if the old man was gone away.

'Ah, dear, then you hadn't heard?' she said, giving her eyes a wipe. 'Well, to be sure, it was only ten days ago, I dare say you wouldn't have. Poor old gentleman.'

'What happened, Mrs Grimes? Did he get ill?'

'No, 'twasn't like that. It was all along of that there crusader's dog up in the church.'

'What happened?' Toby asked again, anxiously.

'Well, Mr Brooman was very upset, dreadful upset he was, on account of the Historical Monuments Department, or some such, sent an inspector along and then they decided as how the old dog shouldn't be left there an' allowed to fall into the sea like all the rest o' the bits from the church, but was to be took off and put into York Museum. Oh, he argued about it terrible, did Mr Brooman, an' ast the vicar and even writ to the Council, but they wouldn't take no notice of him, said it was best that the dog should be preserved because it was an uncommon example of twelfth-century work.'

'Oh, my goodness.' Toby's heart sank dreadfully. He could imagine how Mr Brooman must have felt. 'Did – did they take the dog away?'

'Well, they was all set to. A couple of chaps come out with hammers and chisels and a council van, an' they took the old dog off his base and put him in a crate an' fetched it down here to the village. 'Twas a desprit cold arternoon, snow and wind, an' it must ha' been a sharp old job prying that heavy stone thing loose, up there on the headland. So when they was done they went into the Old Ship for a quick warm-up. And you'll never guess what Mr Brooman did.'

'What did he do?' Toby asked, though he thought he *could* guess.

'Why, he must ha' fetched out his old garden barrer – for bits of it was washed up along the shore next day – an' (no one knows how he done it, all on his own, wi'out help) he must ha' got that crate out o' the van an' into his wheelbarrer and wheeled it down to the sea – wheeled it right *into* the sea. And Doctor Motkin reckons that

musta given him a heart-failure – for he'd had one or two bad turns with his heart already, this last two-three months – anyway, he never came back.' She wiped her eyes again. 'Washed up, he was, next morning, half a mile down the shore. But they say his face was ever so peaceful. Maybe he was glad to go. Arter all, 'tis a long time since his missis died, poor old soul.'

'What about Tob— what about the dog? Did they find him?'

'Never a trace. There's a big undertow here, you know – special when summat's heavy – it must ha' gone right down deep. The Ancient Monuments people were mad about it; terrible put out they were. But there was naught that anyone could do.'

No there wasn't, thought Toby, and he felt proud for old Mr Brooman, battling his way down to the sea through snow and gale. He thought of the old man's voice saying, 'Things that come from the village ought to stay here.'

He thanked Mrs Grimes and went out into the street.

He knew he ought to go home and help his mother – who would be wondering where in the world he had got to – unpack and make the beds and decorate the Christmas tree. But he hadn't the heart to do that, quite yet.

He turned into the biting wind, followed by Harriet, who was rather subdued, and walked along the short snowy street to the beach.

Dusk was falling. As far as the eye could see the beach curved away to right and left, an unbroken sweep of white. And the sea mumbled and muttered, inky black, far out, with a pale frill of foam at its edge. Nobody, nothing was stirring. Even the birds were silent.

But out on that windswept emptiness Harriet's spirits suddenly picked up, and she went bounding off, lifting her feet ridiculously high, with a rocking curvetting motion, like a painted dog. Down to the water's edge she galloped, and splashed in.

Toby raced after her, as fast as he could go – faster – much faster – swallowing great gulps of burning cold air. And as he ran, the sorrow for Mr Brooman's death fell away behind him, and a feeling of freedom and triumph streamed through him – as if he had been joined by the happy spirits of Crusader's Toby and Mr Brooman, old no longer but light and strong as on the day when he had raced with the Olympic torch across the plains of Yugoslavia.